Southern Heart

SPECIAL EDITION

NATASHA MADISON

Dedication: To Erica, my new romance reader. Watching you read book and fall in love with reading is one of the best things to come out of this crazy time.

Someday when the pages of my life end, I know that you will be one of the most beautiful chapters. Anonymous

One

CHELSEA

After putting the truck in park, a smile spreads across my face as I look out at all the trees. "It's good to be home." I get out of the truck and notice the wind has picked up when I hear the leaves rustling in the trees. I spend an extra second just to take it in again. Living in the city, I don't have any of this. I have car horns and sirens.

The blue sky has clouded over, and my blond hair covers my face now. I don't know why, but the air smells so different here than anywhere else. It just smells like home. My black ballerina shoes are no match for the rocks in the driveway, so it's time to dust off the cowboy boots.

I hear the front door open and look up, seeing my brother, Ethan, coming outside. His whole face lights up with a smile. "Well, well, well," he says, coming down the front steps of his house. "If it isn't Care Bear."

I shake my head at the nickname he gave me when I decided to go into nursing. "How long are you going to keep that up?" I ask as he gets closer to me, grabbing me and pulling me close to him.

My hands go around his waist. "Welcome home," he says, putting his chin on top of my head like he always does.

"It's good to be home," I tell him. Five years ago, I decided I would try my hand at being a nurse. I wasn't sure how I would like it, but I fell in love with it and graduated last week at the top of my class.

"Is Mom all over you?" He lets go of me now as we walk into his house.

"Let's just say that I'm happy I have my own house." We both laugh. Even though my parents expected me to move back home and had my bedroom all ready, I needed to have my own space.

"I'm still surprised she went for that." He looks over at me.

"Oh, she didn't at first." I stop when I get up the two steps. "But then I threw in that you disappeared from our lives for five years." When he was twenty-one, he found out that his father was not Jacob. He didn't handle it well and took off for five years, cutting everyone off. It was a rough time for everyone, but he's home now.

"Nice." He pushes my shoulder now.

"Daddy!" Gabriel, his four-year-old son, yells his name and then looks down the hall and sees me here, and his blue eyes sparkle. "Auntie Cece!" he yells, running to me, and I bend down to grab him in my arms. He wraps his arms around my neck and his legs around my waist.

I turn my head to kiss his neck just as I did when he was a baby. "I can't even pick you up." I pretend he's too heavy. No one knows I made the decision to become a nurse because of Gabriel.

One looked at him and I fell so madly in love with him I couldn't explain it. I also got this fear he would get sick, and I wouldn't be able to actually help him. "Have you been eating your vegetables?"

"I did." He squirms to get out of my embrace, and I see

he's really gotten big since the last time I saw him six months ago. "Feel my muscles." He puts up his hand, and I squeeze it.

"I think you are even bigger than your dad." Bending to kiss him on the neck and blow bubbles in his neck. He squeals out in delight, and it's music to my ears.

"Chelsea." I hear my name being called and look up to see my sister-in-law, Emily, coming toward us with a baby on her hip. The smile on her face matches Ethan's.

My one-year-old niece, Aubrey, chews on her finger while she looks at me and smiles. "Well, hello there, pretty girl." I take her from Emily, and she claps her hands, showing me her gummy smile.

"You look fabulous," she says to me. "I love those jeans." I nod, looking down at the black jeans I put on today with a white shirt and short black leather jacket. City chic but also okay for the country. "What are you doing here?" Emily asks, and I just look at her.

"I'm here to babysit my two favorite people in the whole world," I tell her, looking at my brother. "Someone called and begged and pleaded."

"I did not beg or plead," Ethan says, walking to Emily and putting his arm around her shoulders.

"He said he's naming the next baby after me." I wink at her, and they both laugh now.

"I just made her feel just a touch guilty that she hasn't put Aubrey to bed in six months," he says, turning now and walking into the house.

"Ethan," Emily says his name. "She just got back two days ago." I knew that the minute I graduated, I would be going back home. I did my training in one of the busiest hospitals in the state. I went from the emergency room to surgery to obstetrics to see what I really wanted, and in the end, I just loved the emergency trauma. It pushed me on so many levels and I found it challenging. It also gave me a chance to work with different doctors. No matter how much I loved the hustle and bustle, I knew I wanted to come back home.

"And she is bored out of her mind." He repeats what I told him. "She said it herself."

"I did," I say. I reached out to one of the top medical centers in the area, and I start in a month. I could have started right away, but I wanted to get settled and have some extra family time, seeing my cousins and my grandmother. But I was getting antsy to get back out there. "I might call and ask if I can start before I'm scheduled."

We walk into the house, and I see toys scattered everywhere. I look around the living room, but everything is much the same. The only thing is the new family pictures that Emily keeps adding. I pick up a frame on the side table, seeing the picture of all of us at Christmas. "I see that someone really put his foot down with no more toys."

"Don't look at me," Ethan says, walking to grab a glass. "It's all Emily."

"I can't even believe you just said that." She looks at him. "You, Mr. McIntyre, are fibbing." She folds her arms over her chest. "Now I'm going to take a shower and even put on jeans."

"Jeans are overrated," I say. "They also judge you. Don't listen to them."

"You're wearing jeans." She points at my pants.

"I was in nursing school and working at the hospital. I lived on coffee and ramen noodles. Sometimes I ate the noodles uncooked." She walks back to their bedroom as I sit on the couch next to Aubrey. She is lying down, watching some cartoon playing on the big-screen television. I kiss the top of her head, and she looks up and smiles at me.

Forty-five minutes later, Ethan is opening the car door for Emily. "There is a bottle in the fridge already," Emily says, sticking her head out of the window. "They both ate, so bath time in an hour, and then they should go right to bed."

"I know the drill," I say, standing on the porch holding Gabriel's hand with Aubrey on my hip.

"Call if you need us," Ethan says. "And by that, I mean we will see you later."

"Wave bye," I tell the kids as they drive away from the house.

I look up at the sky now and see that the clouds are rolling in faster and faster. Gone is the blue sky and the fluffy white clouds. The sky darkens with gray clouds, and I feel a couple of drops. "I smell rain," I say to Gabriel as we turn to walk back into the house before the sky opens up and the pouring rain starts. "Now, how about you show me all your favorite toys?"

"Yes," Gabriel says, jumping up and down. He pulls my hand toward his playroom in the back of the house. The floor-to-ceiling windows view the backyard and the big pool Ethan put in right next to the enormous play structure the guys spent a weekend building last year. The worn hammock remains in the yard. No matter how tattered it gets, they refuse to get rid of it.

Placing Aubrey down, I sit on the plush beige carpet in the middle of the room. Gabriel goes on and on about all of his toys while Aubrey brings me one doll after another. I kiss her sweet little cheeks every single time. When she finally brings her last doll over, she turns and sits in the middle of my legs, gibbering the whole time. I've missed so much by not being home, but watching these two grow up is what I missed the most.

Even though I saw them during our regular FaceTime sessions, it's not the same. I hear the rain start, and I look outside the window and see that the dark clouds have taken over. "It's raining cats and dogs," Gabriel says, and I laugh at him, knowing Grandma taught him that.

"Why don't we go take a nice bubble bath?" We clean up the room, then I walk back to their bathroom. By the time they've finished their bath, I have to put down four towels to clean up our splashing. I tie my hair on top of my head as I dress them both and then walk back into the kitchen to warm a bottle up.

While I wait for the microwave to beep, a huge clap of thunder makes me jump. I laugh, thinking I'm being silly. Rainstorms are my favorite, but I don't like the thunder and lightning that go along with them. "That was a big one." I look out the kitchen window but can't see anything since the rain is coming down so hard.

I'm rocking Aubrey to sleep when thunder claps again, and this time, I see the lightning through the windows.

The lights flicker, but the kids are oblivious to the fact a storm is raging outside. I place her in bed and check on Gabriel, who is fast asleep.

I close his door just a touch and walk back to the living room starting to clean up when the lights flicker again. I walk to the kitchen, looking for candles in case the lights go out.

The lightning outside is intense this time. It lights up the whole sky, the rain not letting up, and now it sounds as if little pellets are hitting the windows. I find the candle at the same time I hear a soft ticking. *Tick. Tick. Tick.*

I look around, walking to the back door to make sure it's locked as another round of lightning starts, this time with a roaring sound of thunder first. "Someone is getting their asses kicked tonight." I walk toward the front door, where I can still hear the ticking.

A tree branch is swaying from the wind and hitting the front window. I turn off most of the lights and sit down when it sounds like two rocks being crushed together fills the whole house, and the lights go out.

"Great," I say to myself, getting up. I'm ready to send

Ethan a text to tell him that we are fine when the thunder starts again, but this time, there is also banging on the door.

I drop the phone as my hands go to my chest. Making my way through the darkness, I slowly head to the front door. The streaks of lightning give me some light as I get to the door and look out the peephole.

All I see is a black lump. My head screams at me not to open the door while my hands reach out my hand going to the lock and turning it.

I start to pull it open, and it's pushed in by someone bent over. I scream, not sure what to do. The lightning gives me just enough light to see that the man is bloody. His face is bruised and battered, and he has blood everywhere along with dirt. His dirty white shirt is soaked through from the rain, and parts of his shirt are pink from the blood. My heart pounds in my chest, the fear creeping in as I look to turn and grab the kids. I back away from him as he crashes into the table in the hallway, the vase of flowers crashing down now at the same time as the thunder strikes again.

He holds up one hand, and I can see the dripping blood. "Oh my god."

"Help." It's the only thing he says to me before falling to the floor in front of me.

Two

MAYSON

"Help." It comes out in a whisper as my legs finally give out on me, and I fall to the floor. My knees hitting it with a whack at the same time as another clap of thunder fills the air.

"Oh my god," I hear the woman say, and I try to see her, but everything is blurry. I lift my hand, but it just falls to the floor when the darkness starts to suck me under.

"Ethan," she says his name frantically as I try to place the voice. "Ethan, someone just came to the house. He's bloody, and he's lying on the floor. He's not in good shape." The sound of rain fills the room, and I can see the flickers of lightning as I try to make my way back up to the surface.

I hear her running around, and I wonder what she's doing when I hear the door close with a slam, making her yell and the phone clatter to the floor. "It's okay," I try to tell her, but the only thing that comes out is a moan.

I feel her beside me, then she rolls me over to my back, and a gasp escapes her. "Can you hear me?" She leans over me, and I want to tell her I hear her, but nothing comes out.

All the adrenaline coursing through me from the past

three hours suddenly wears off, leaving me in a heap in the middle of Ethan's house.

Crawling in the middle of darkness, I scan the area until I know where the path opens. Finding the tree big enough to take cover in, I slowly rise to my feet, ignoring the slicing pain in both legs from where he stabbed me. My body molds to the tree as I swallow, and the sky opens up in a downpour. The water falls through the trees right on me, soaking the shirt on my back and causing my jeans to mold to me. I take a step forward, and my knees give out on me. "I will not die here," I tell the universe as soon as the thunder claps back.

"There is blood everywhere," the voice says, and I have to wonder if anyone else is with her. "Who are you?" she asks me, and I can only imagine the state of my face with the dirt and grime mixed with the blood that is surely pouring out of my cuts.

"May..." I start to say, but another roll of thunder comes through, and the darkness chases it.

She picks up my arm, her fingers going to my pulse. "It's barely there."

"I'm right here!" I scream at her, but nothing comes out. Not even a groan this time.

"I'm right here," I chant over and over again, but this time my body fades further and further away from her voice. "I'm right here."

Three

CHELSEA

Lightning strikes again as he looks up at me with one eye. The other one is swollen shut. His mouth tries to move, but no sounds come out. His arm comes up again and then crashes down.

My heart hammers in my chest as I find the source of the blood. His white shirt is soaked with a big red stain on his side, and I pull it up to see he's wounded there. "Can you hear me?" I ask him, my voice shaking as I take deep breaths to stay calm. I lift his shirt higher and see he's got bruising but no other open wounds. He has one piece of cloth tied around his leg, and his legs have bloodstains on them, too. Hearing the sound of rocks crunching under tires makes me look up. The wind blows through here, slamming the front door, and I look around to make sure I don't see Gabriel.

The lights flicker on and off again as I hear a car door. I wonder if the person who put him in this state is coming to finish the job.

Fear creeps into me, making me get up now, and I look around the house, wondering where he keeps the gun, but I don't have to look far before the door swings open. Ethan stands there soaked to the bone, the gun drawn in his arms, aiming it at the person on the floor. "Chelsea," he says my name as lightning flashes behind him.

"I'm okay," I tell him right away. "The kids are okay."

"What the fuck?" he says, looking at the man on the floor in front of him. I look at his chest, hoping to see movement, and it rises and falls so slowly that if you aren't focused, you would think he was dead.

"There was a banging on the door," I start to tell him, and the tears pour out of me, and I just let them fall as the fear now leaves my body, knowing that Ethan is here. "And then..." I start to talk, but the man on the floor moans.

"You opened the door to a stranger?" he shouts at me, and I glare at him now.

"Are you fucking kidding me right now?" I hiss at him, and the man holds his side. "How the hell was I supposed to know?"

"Ethan." He calls my brother's name, and my brother's face goes white as he bends next to him. He looks the man up and down and then focuses on the man's arms. Picking one up, he washes the dirt off him with his shirt. "Ethan." He repeats his name in almost a whisper. I've heard this voice before, I think to myself. I know I have, but with the thunder and the monsoon of rain coming down, I can't focus.

"It's Mayson," he says, his voice frantic. My stomach drops, and Emily comes into the house with the phone at her ear. My hand goes to my mouth now as I look down at the beaten man in front of me. He is covered in dirt and blood, and if I didn't know better, I'd think he crawled here on his hands and knees. I think back to the first time I met him.

"Chelsea." My brother, Ethan, called my name clear across the field and I walked over without thinking twice about it. Only when I got closer did my heart speed up as I looked at the guy standing beside my brother. He was just as tall, maybe even a

11

touch taller. He was definitely bigger than Ethan was. His arms bulged out more, his chest wider. The tattoos on his arms shining orange in the sunlight. "This," he tells the guy next to him, "is my baby sister."

"Younger sister," I corrected him. "Harlow is your baby sister," I reminded him and he laughed as he shook his head. "This is Carey." He said his name and then corrected himself, "Sorry, Mayson."

I smiled at this stranger in front of me, and he smiled obligatory at me. "Nice to meet you."

The sunglasses hid his brown eyes. My heart sped up as he took my hand in his and it felt like an electric shock ran through me, all the way to my bones. It was also the day I secretly started my crush on him.

"It's your dad." Emily's eyes look around the room, seeing the vase on the floor shattered.

"Tell him to get here and bring the men," Ethan says and looks at me. "You have to help him."

I look at him, shocked. "Help him." I turn now and run to the bathroom, grabbing all the towels and tossing them in the sink. I turn on the water, my hands shaking as much as the leaves outside in the storm. Emily runs into the bathroom, her whole body soaked, mud all over her floor as she looks at me, and I let a sob go. I put my hand to my mouth to try to block the noise of the sobs that come. I was so scared that something was going to happen to the kids. I didn't think of anything else but making sure the kids were okay.

"It's okay," she says, coming to me and hugging me. The wetness of her body soaks into my chest.

"The kids?" I ask nervously, looking around her as I rub the tears off my face.

"Sleeping," she says as she cups my cheek. "They're safe and don't even know what's going on."

"I was so scared," I tell her. "So scared I wouldn't be able to protect the kids. I'm so sorry, Emily. I should never have opened the door." The guilt of the kids being hurt because of me is so much more than I can say. "I would never have."

"Chelsea," Emily says my name softly. "There is no one else in this world I trust more with my children than you."

I swallow down the other sob that wants to rip through me. "Good," I say, grabbing the towel from the sink and wringing it in my hands. Trying to be strong at this moment, I shake my head and push away the fear I had. "I need you to get me a basin with warm water," I tell her, "and I need a pair of scissors." I look around, bending to open the cabinets under the sink. "Do you have a first aid kit?" I ask her, and she nods at me. "Bring it to me." I squeeze the extra water out of the towels. Grabbing them all in my hands, I walk back into the room.

Ethan is kneeling beside Mayson, and I kneel beside him. "I'm going to clean your face now," I tell Mayson even though he can't hear me, and slowly wipe his face with one of the wet towels. The mud is coming off easier than I thought. "You need stitches in your cheek." The gash on his cheek is now leaking blood, and I apply a bit of pressure to stop the bleeding. "Hold this on his cheek," I tell Ethan, and he puts his hand on the towel. I ignore the pain in my chest as I wipe away the dirt from his swollen eye. One towel isn't enough to clean just his face. Emily comes in with the bucket of warm water and places it beside me, then she hands me the first aid kit. I open it and grab the gauze, pushing it on his gunshot wound. "I need more towels," I tell her, and she gets up.

Emily rushes out of the room and grabs another one as Ethan just looks at me in shock. "He needs stitches on his cheek and his forehead." I look down at the shirt and look up at Ethan, who nods his head at me. "He's been shot." I look at Ethan, and my eyes go to the wound. He picks up one of Mayson's hands, and I see the raw and bloody marks around his wrists. My eyes find the ink on his arm I've spent so much time studying from afar.

Ethan lifts Mayson's shirt, and I see the bullet wound as the squishing sound of the shirt being torn away from the wound is heard. My eyes focus on the wound. "Chelsea," Ethan says my name, and I snap into action.

"I need my bag." I look up at Emily, who has tears rolling down her face as she watches Mayson fight for his life. She turns and runs out into the rainstorm. I grab his wrist in my hand and feel for a pulse. "It's steady but..."

I look up toward the open door when headlights shine into the house. The crunching of rocks sounds under tires as someone parks their truck. Two doors open and close, then I hear running but look down when I hear moaning again. I see his finger twitch.

"What the fuck happened?" I hear from beside me and look up to see my cousin Quinn walking in with his father and our uncle Casey, and both of them are drenched. Quinn carries my black medical bag while Casey has his arm around Emily. The bag was a gift from my grandparents when I graduated and has a gold monogram of my name stitched on the side.

"I have no idea," I start to say. "He came here, banging on the door." I open my bag and look over at Ethan. "What is the ETA on the ambulance?" Ethan ignores my eyes and turns to look at Casey.

"No." We hear grumbling coming from Mayson, and my eyes go back down to him as he tries to shake his head from side to side.

"If he came here," Ethan says, "then he's running from someone."

"If he's running," Casey says, stepping forward, "then we need to get him the fuck out of here. Far away from here."

Ethan nods his head and looks at me. "What can you do to make him comfortable so we can take him out of here?"

"Take him out of here?" I open the bag and grab my stethoscope. "Are you insane? He needs a hospital. First off, he's been shot. Then his legs need to be checked out. I don't even know what is going on internally. He can have a head injury we don't know about. He needs a hospital."

"He had to have been in his right mind to drive here." Ethan looks at me, and I want to agree with him.

"Any normal person wouldn't be able to walk ten steps with his injuries," I say. "You guys are trained for this," I tell him. "You're trained to shut it down and fight through everything until you get to your hub." I throw up my hand. "Or whatever it's called."

"Chelsea," Casey says my name, and I look up at my uncle, who now squats down in front of us. "Honey, he can't go to the hospital. Ethan is right."

"You are all insane." I shake my head. "I will get him as stable as I can, and then his doctor can treat him."

Ethan looks at Casey, and the two share a look. "Honey," my uncle Casey says, and I know what is coming. But even if I know it's coming, hearing the words makes me shake my head. "You can treat him."

"Are you two crazy?" I look at them both and then up at Quinn, who is looking at me. Nothing is on his face but worry. "I can't do this." I get up, waiting for someone else to say how fucking crazy this is. Quinn now averts his eyes, and when I look at Emily, she wrings her hands.

Emily steps forward now. "If anyone can help him, you can." She comes to me and puts her hand in mine.

"I'm a nurse. I am not a doctor. He might need surgery, and that is not even my specialty." I look down now as my eyes focus on the bullet wound. It's leaking down his side to the floor, where there is a puddle of blood now. "An X-ray needs to be done to make sure I know where the bullet is lodged. We need to get him hydrated."

"I can get anything you need," Casey says, "except the X-ray machine."

"Bullet..." We hear from Mayson, and all eyes turn back to him as he hisses through the pain, using all of his energy as he says the next words. His eye close as he starts to talk again. But he stays alert enough to tell us everything. "Went straight through." I grab a pair of gloves from my bag. "My legs." I look down and see the seeping, soaked pant legs that I didn't even notice. "Stabbed four times." He trails off now, and we know because his head turns to the side. My head spins when I think of his wounds and how the injuries point to his hands being tied. My eyes fly to Ethan's. He's looking at me, knowing what I'm going to say next.

"This wasn't just a five-minute thing," I say to the whole room. "He was tortured," I whisper, looking at him. He doesn't have a chance to answer me because two car doors slam, and everyone looks toward the front door. The rain has finally slowed.

My father, Beau, and Ethan's father, Jacob, run up the stairs. Both of their eyes assess the situation. My father finds my eyes right away, making sure I'm okay, and then he looks down at Mayson.

"Did he attack you?" he asks, confused by this whole scene.

"I'll fill you in, Uncle Beau," Quinn says. "But first, we need to get him over to Chelsea's house."

"My house?" I snap. "Why my house?" My heartbeat is going so fast now it echoes in my ears.

"Now wait a second," my father snaps, stepping forward and holding up his hands to stop everyone. "We are not bringing him to her house."

"This needs to be under the radar," Ethan says to him. "I

would never ever put her in harm's way, but we need someone who can monitor him."

"Then hire someone." I stand and take off my gloves. "Just like Uncle Casey can get whatever I need, I'm sure you can get a doctor who can take care of him."

"Honey," Jacob says, looking at me. "I don't think anyone can take care of him as well as you can. If it came down to it, there is no one I would want except you."

"You took an oath," Ethan says, and I glare at him.

I then say the words that shock not only everyone in this room but even me. "Get him in the truck."

Four

MAYSON

"Get him in the truck." I hear Chelsea's voice, and try to open my eyes, but one is sealed shut. The other one is blurry from the sweat and blood dripping off my forehead. I try to lift my hand, but nothing happens. Not even a twitch. I focus on what is going on around me. I can hear everything, and I want them to know, but I can't communicate with them. "Someone needs to apply pressure on his bullet wound to make sure he doesn't lose anymore blood," Chelsea says, and I hear people move all around me. "I need a belt," she yells, "to tie around his legs to stop the blood flow until we get him back to my house!"

"Be careful moving him," Ethan says as the men lift me, and the pain rips through me. My stab wounds in my legs feel like they are ripping open. The bullet wound in my side feels like someone lit a match and put it straight inside it. In my head, I'm roaring out in pain, but in reality, the only thing that comes out of me is a groan. "We've got you, Mayson," I hear Ethan say from beside me. Ethan and his family are the only ones who call me Mayson. Everyone else uses Carey, my last name, and I don't know why, but it's only when I hear those

18

words does my body let go. The tension leaves, and I soak into the darkness.

"Come here, you fucking piece of shit." His voice came out in a snarl as his spit flew on my face, and he grasped my hair in his fist. "You thought you saw the last of me." He chuckled as he grabbed my chin in his hand as hard as he could, squeezing. "Hiding like a fucking coward." I looked into the eyes that I prayed I would never see again. Eyes that haunted my dreams.

Letting my chin go, I knew pain would come next, and I was not wrong when he kicked me right in the ribs. One. Two. Three. He always went for three. My hands were tied together around a tree in the middle of the forest.

I closed my eyes, trying to focus on anything but the pain, and it was just too much for him. "Oh, no, you don't." He grabbed my hair into his fist, pulling my head back. "Not yet, you fucker." He smiled as he looked at me. "You close your eyes when I tell you to," he said, shocking me when he head-butted me.

"We will place him on the flatbed," Chelsea says. "I'm going to ride in the back with him to make sure he's stable." I feel myself being carried. "It's pitch black. I need a flashlight," she tells Ethan, and I can tell she is irritated with him. I've been around her a total of ten times, and each time, I've learned something new about her. But I got her irritated look after ten minutes.

"It's a four-minute ride if we use the backroads," Jacob says as I feel the cold metal of the truck against my back.

"Don't let go of the pressure on his side," Chelsea says to someone. "Don't you fucking die on me," I hear her whisper in my ear.

I don't know how long it takes, but when the truck finally stops, my stomach roils. I'm carried off the truck and then placed on the softest bed and sheets I've ever been on. I know that I'm going to owe her a new bed when this is all over. If I survive, that is.

"I can see bruising on his ribs," I hear Chelsea say, and my breathing starts to come in short spurts as the pain races through me. "Of course we can't know because I have nothing here."

"You can't do anything for broken ribs anyway," Ethan says, and I can feel the glare Chelsea gives him. "What? It's true."

"Well, I'm assuming he didn't puncture his lung since he isn't choking on his own blood," she hisses out.

"Jesus, Chels," Ethan says.

"Is Casey back with the stuff I need?" she asks, and then I feel her hands on me. Soft and cool. "It's becoming infected," she says, touching the gunshot wound.

"Hey." I hear another voice, and I go on alert until I hear Ethan call his name.

"What's up, Quinn?" My eyes open just a sliver, and I see Quinn standing there looking like he just ran a fucking marathon and didn't stop.

"I got his truck taken care of," he says. "Dad has his burner phone and is going through it. We are also leaving crumbs, so if someone comes after him, we'll know."

I try to move my hand, and then I feel her hand go into mine. "Mayson," she says, and I turn my head as fast as I can. I see her faintly as I try to open my eyes. Her hair is piled on her head now. "It's Chelsea." She blinks away the tears that I know are coming. "You're safe. We have you." I squeeze her hand and then try to open my eye, and I see her blue eyes looking at me with her smile. "Hi," she says, sniffling back.

"Water," I say in a harsh whisper, and she looks over at Ethan, who is bringing me water with a straw.

"Take small sips," Chelsea says, and I take a small sip, my

mouth dry and feels like sand is on my tongue. Must be from when I crawled through the forest.

"Not," I start to say, "my truck." My tongue is so heavy, and my throat feels like I have cotton balls shoved down it.

"Don't waste your energy," Ethan says when Casey walks into the room with two bags in his hands. "We have time for that later."

"I'm not even going to ask how you got all the stuff I asked for in less than"—Chelsea looks at her watch—"twenty-seven minutes."

"It's better that way," Casey says and walks over to me. "We have you covered, and you're in good hands."

I nod my head, and I want to stay up talking, but I feel a prick in my arm and see Chelsea look at me. "That should relax you and hopefully put you under. I'll try to be as gentle as I can."

"Do your worst," I say, right before my eye closes, and I sink into the darkness. Yet I hear everything happening around me.

"Okay, Ethan," she says softly. "I'm going to need your hands."

"Whatever you need," he says, and I know that if I die right here, he would honor me with respect and dignity—two things I don't think I'm worthy of and never did. I try to stay alert. Try to use the tools I found in the Army, but I can't fight it anymore and just sink even deeper back to relive the terror of the past five days.

"Wake up, you son of a bitch. I'm not done with you yet." He slapped my face with all his force, causing the back of my head to hit the tree. "No good for nothing. You die when I tell you it's time to die." With shot after shot, I tasted metal in my mouth, but I shut it out. Once the blows stopped, I counted the steps, forty steps, and I knew he was sitting in my cabin. My fucking cabin. It was only when I counted to one hundred that I knew he wasn't

coming back and started to hatch a plan. My hands were tied, and I had rope burn around my wrists. I fought through it until I heard a noise. He tried to sneak up on me, but the branches snapped under his boots, and I had one second before he plunged the knife into my leg.

I gasp out, and my eye opens. One is still sealed shut as I look around the lit room. My heart is beating so fast in my chest, and my breathing is coming out in pants. With one sweep around the room, I remember where I am. I try to lift my hand, but it's still so heavy. I blink my eye again, trying to focus and fight off the darkness pulling me under. Ethan looks at me right away, his eyes relaying he's got my back. "Where am I?" I mumble, trying like hell to leave my eye open.

"Somewhere safe." Ethan comes over to me, and I try to swallow. "Chelsea is going to take care of you. All you need to do is hang in there."

There is so much I want to tell him in case I don't survive, so many secrets I've buried, but some secrets have a way of coming back and haunting us, no matter how much we try to bury them. I look into Ethan's eyes. "Save your energy for after," he tells me. "There is time for all the answers."

The darkness comes now and sucks me into the hell that I lived.

All I saw was the dark sky, always the dark sky. It could be because the trees were so dense that no sunlight could come through. My favorite time of year was when hardly no one came up here. But I knew these woods like the back of my hand. I studied them, I guess, for this moment. "I'll fucking kill you," he spat in my face, stabbing me one more time in the leg. I swallowed down the pain and refused to let him see it. If I was going to die, it was going to be without giving him any fucking satisfaction.

"Then do it already." I looked at him. His white shirt had rust-colored stains, and I knew it was my blood that had dried.

"Pussy." I egged him on. Except for this time, he snarled at me and dropped the knife right next to my feet.

I took my eyes off him for one second, and it was in that second that he put his hand behind his back and brought out the gun. "Pussy this," he said right before he shot me, and I blacked out again.

"Fuck." I hear Chelsea's voice, and I want to say I'm awake, but I can't because the darkness comes again. "His blood pressure is dropping."

"You're nothing." I heard him right beside me. "Fucking nothing but a worthless piece of shit." He kicked me and walked away. I waited until I knew he was gone before opening my eye and looking at the spot where he dropped the knife. It took everything in me to move my legs to drag the knife to me. I worked with cutting my hands free. The pain in my side had me seeing stars. I waited until the darkness had filled the trees, knowing full well he would probably not come out. I waited to gather my strength until I could make my escape.

I didn't know how long I had. I didn't know what day it was. I didn't know what time it was. The only thing I knew was that I wasn't going to fucking die here. Not today.

Five

CHELSEA

"Showtime," I tell them and turn around, grabbing a pair of gloves and my scissors. I get close to him, and only then do I see how dirty he is. His jeans have dried mud on them. I start cutting up the pants on one leg and then the other, then peel the pants from his legs, but the dried blood pulls his skin. He moans out in pain when it pulls and a couple of the wounds open. "Fuck," I say and look down at his legs. "Five open wounds," I say and then cut his shirt up the middle.

His white shirt is now a dusty brown, and the part where he was shot is a rusty color. "Okay, let's see what happened here." I pull the shirt, and the stickiness of the blood sticks to the white shirt. "I need to see if it really came out the back." I look at Ethan, who just nods at me. He lifts him by the side, and I see the exit wound. "Well, it went right through." I walk over to the bag Casey brought in that is now laid out on top of the desk in the room. My hands start to shake a bit as I doubt myself.

"Chelsea." Quinn calls my name, and I look at him. He is one of my best friends in the world and my cousin. He also knows me better than most people. "You graduated at the top of your class for a reason." I just nod at him as he turns and walks out of the room. Casey comes to stand in front of the bed.

"What can I do to help?" he asks, stepping forward to watch what I'm doing.

"I need you to be my right-hand person when I need something," I say, looking down at the gunshot wound. I've only ever seen one gunshot wound in my whole career. The last time, I was an intern, so all I had to do was watch. I look up at Mayson, seeing his one eye sealed shut and already purple. Even though I washed his face at Ethan's, it's still streaked with mud. I look over to see that Ethan is dragging the desk to me now, and Casey has turned and walked out of the room. I lean down and whisper in his ear, "Don't you fucking die on me, Mayson." I stand now and close my eyes. Looking up, I see my father standing in the doorway. "I'm good."

"Oh, I know you are," he says. "You got that from your mother," he says with tears in his eyes. My uncle Jacob stands beside him with his arms folded over his chest, smirking at me. He usually does that when he knows I'm about to show everyone when I'm boss. It started when I was a kid, and Quinn bet me that I couldn't ride the mechanical bull as long as him. Well, he was wrong. I rode it longer. Forget that I broke my arm to prove him wrong.

"I got the water," Casey says to me, and I look over to see him carrying a white bin with warm water.

"Let's get the party started." I say that every single time I get a trauma. I put an IV in him with a bag of saline to keep him hydrated. "I need something to hold up the IV fluid." I look at Quinn, and he nods at me, turning and walking out of the room as Jacob walks in, carrying an ECG machine. My mouth hangs open as I look at both of them.

"So I'm supposed to believe that you having an ECG machine just lying around the barn?" They both share a look.

"Like that's normal." I walk over and hook Mayson up. Placing the gray peg on his finger. The machine starts to monitor his heartbeat. "It's slow," I tell them. "But steady."

"At least it's beating," Ethan says. "Here." He hands me the blue surgical cover, and I look down at my shirt, seeing that his blood is all over me. I slip my hands in and slip on another pair of clean gloves. I turn, and everything else fades away. I block out everyone in the room and the only thing I focus on is Mayson. Quinn comes back in with a stick and a hanger. Tying it to the side of the bed, he hangs up the saline bag.

I clean off the wound as gently as I can and look up to see if he wakes up. When I don't see his eyes flutter, I continue seeing to the bullet hole. The whole time, questions are going through my head. Who would do this to him? Why would they do this to him? Where did he crawl out from? How long was he kept? From the look at the welts on his wrists, he was held captive for days. When was the last time someone spoke to him? How long would he have been missing before someone asked questions? My head swirls as I make sure the wound is clean before I grab the hook and some thread.

My stomach burns as I think of him alone out there with no one knowing he was missing. My parents text me twice a day, and if I don't answer them, they have a phone chain they put into effect. How does he not have this? Why doesn't he have this? Who is this man who has slowly crept into my family?

"How is his pressure?" I ask Ethan, who had this training when he was in the black ops team.

"Normal," he says. "How's the wound?"

"Normal." I smirk at him and bend my head to start stitching him up.

~

I HANG MY HEAD DOWN AND LET THE WATER cascade around me. The tightness in my neck doesn't go away. I've been up for thirty-eight hours straight, give or take. Watching the water swirl down the drain, I'm fixated on that image and trying to forget everything I just saw.

Closing my eyes, all I can see is blood. So much fucking blood I didn't think he would make it, and all I could do was ignore the way my heart was beating. I had to ignore the fear that was creeping in and focus on keeping him alive. Everyone helped in their own way, but no one could have stitched him up like me. So I refused to even take a break. I refused to drink. I refused everything until the last stitch was sewn, and were there ever fucking stitches.

Seventy stitches just on his legs and twenty for the bullet wound. I close my hands, looking down at them, and then the cramping starts.

I turn off the water and step out of the shower, grabbing the white towel. Wrapping it around myself, I slip on a pair of yoga pants and a T-shirt. I tie my hair on top of my head, ignoring the tension in the back of my neck that is not going away.

Opening the bathroom door, I'm shocked when I see my mother sitting on the bed. "Mom," I say her name, and she turns to look at me. "What are you doing here?" I ask. I'm suddenly scared he coded, and no one came to get me. She sees my eyes moving from her to the door and back to her.

"Dad called me." She smiles at me. "I brought over something for you to eat." She points at the tray of food she placed on the bedside table. I let out a huge sigh of relief.

"Where is everyone?" I look toward the hallway, knowing that Ethan is probably sitting by his bed.

"Only Ethan is left," she says, and I go and sit next to her. "You need to sleep."

"I need to eat and sleep but," I say, looking toward the door, "he needs to be watched for the next twenty-four hours."

"And Ethan is with him," she reinterates. "So eat and then get at least four hours of sleep."

Grabbing the tray, I bring it on the bed with us. "Is this Grandma's special soup?"

"Obviously," she says. "We had to talk her and Grandpa down, or they would have charged in here." I laugh, grabbing the spoon, taking a sip of the butternut squash soup that is my favorite.

"It was scary, Mom," I tell her without looking up as I blink away my tears.

She puts her arms around me as I sniffle. "Dad said you were a rock star."

I take a bite of the chicken salad sandwich with fresh cranberries. "He has to say that. He's my dad." I look over at her. "He also paid a shit ton for my education, so he has to say that. I'm exhausted," I say to her, and I hear footsteps from the hallway and look up to see Ethan. "Is he okay?" I'm already getting out of bed to go to him.

"He's fine," he says, looking at me. "I was checking on you."

"I'm fine," I say. "I'm not the one fighting to live."

"You kicked ass, Care Bear," he says, smirking.

"It's not like I had a choice in the matter." I look at them both, and my mother gets off the bed. "You threw me in the deep end and said swim."

"Okay, it's time for me to go and for you to get some rest," my mother says, picking up the tray and turning to me. "Call me if you want to talk."

"Um," I say something and stop. "Is there any chance that the guy who did that...?" I point at the room where Mayson lies.

"Uncle Casey got the guys to come in and wire this place like Fort Knox," Ethan says. "Besides, I'm in the next room."

I slip into bed as he closes the bedroom door, and I sink into the mattress. Pulling up the thick white cover to my neck, I let sleep take over me.

The darkness sucked me in, and I couldn't move. I looked around, and I was in the forest behind my grandparents' house. Looking around as if I was lost, I saw something from the side, and fear crept into me. I felt myself running through the forest, the sounds of branches snapping under my feet.

The echoes of my breathing filled the silence of the darkness. Low tree leaves slapped against legs as I heard someone chant my name. "Chelsea." I looked over my shoulder, the shadow coming closer and closer like a wolf in the night.

I tripped over a log, falling on my face, and the pain hit my stomach right away. I got up and looked down at myself and saw the blood seeping out of my stomach. I put my hand to the side as I felt the burning right through me, then holding it up and seeing the blood all over my hand. "Chelsea." I heard my name yelled frantically, and I turned to see Mayson crawling through the mud. "Run!" he shouted at me, and I turned to run only to be staring into the barrel of a gun.

"You can't run anywhere," he said, holding up his gun. I stared down the barrel of the gun and saw the bullet come right toward me.

Right before the bullet hits me, my eyes fly open, and my hand flies to my chest, rising and falling as if I really did run. I sit up in bed and look down at my side. "It was just a dream," I say to myself. "Just a dream."

Six

MAYSON

"Beep, beep, beep," I hear softly, and I try to pry my eyes open. I'm expecting the darkness to come and take me again, but it doesn't

The light comes in, and I close my eyes again, trying to swallow, and my mouth feels like I swallowed a handful of cotton balls. I move my fingers and then my toes before I look around the room. A cast-iron bed sits in the middle of the room with me in it.

The white covers are up to my waist as I look to the side and see the ECG machine monitoring me. I try to get up, and the pain slices through me, and I hiss out. "You are going to tear your stitches." I hear a voice, and it all comes rushing back to me.

Showing up at Ethan's and collapsing on Chelsea. Them carrying me. "Where am I?" I say in a hoarse voice. My throat burning. "Water."

I see Chelsea get up from the chair in the corner and walk over to me. Her eyes look tired. Her hair is piled on her head. "Hey there, how are you feeling?" She grabs the glass of water beside the bed and offers me the straw.

I take a sip and look down and see that my arms are clean. "Like I got hit by a Mack truck." My throat hurts. "Front and back."

"Well, I hate to say it, but that guy would be better off than you were," she says to me, and she takes her stethoscope off her neck and puts it in her ears. "I'm just going to get your vitals." She grabs the chest piece of her stethoscope and places it in the middle of my chest. I look down at her small hand as she moves it around. She puts them around her neck, and I know it's out of habit.

I don't say anything to her because all the words get stuck in my throat. She grabs a pad from the side table and writes down numbers. "What's the damage?" I try to stretch my legs, but the tightness in them makes me wince.

"Blood pressure is high, but given the fact that you were shot, that is normal," she says, and I see the IV line inside my hand now. "What do you want to know?" She puts down the pad, and I look at her.

She's always been beautiful. The first time I came by to deliver Ethan's things he left behind, I was struck by her beauty. I was also struck by the innocence in her eyes. I also knew she was off-limits in so many ways. "You're a doctor?" I say, and she shakes her head.

"I'm a nurse," she says. "Ethan wants me to call him when you're up." She grabs her phone, texting him now.

"Where am I?" I ask her, and she looks at me.

"My spare bedroom," she says. "They brought you here. You were in and out of it."

"How long have I been out?" I ask, seeing the sun straining to come into the shades. I imagine it's been a couple of hours. I got here during the night, so I must have been out at least six hours.

"Since the last time, sixteen hours," she says, and I'm shocked. "Since you showed up, two weeks."

31

"Two weeks," I say, shocked, my mind going around and around as I think about it.

"You kept coming in and out of it," she tells me, and I wonder if I said anything. "Twitched a couple of times, but other than that, you were good." She sits down on the stool beside my bed, and I look over at the desk with all the tools you would have in a hospital. "I have to say, I didn't know if you were going to make it."

I nod my head. "I didn't see the white light, so I'm assuming it was all peachy."

"If you died in my house." She puts her phone back in her pocket. "There would be hell to pay." She tries to joke, but I can see the seriousness in her eyes as she looks down and then tucks her hair behind her ear. From the first time I met Chelsea, I was pulled to her, but the fact that I was too old and that she was off-limits made me watch her from afar.

"I'll remember that if I see the light." I close my eyes now. "Why am I so tired?"

"Your body suffered major injuries," she says. "To be honest, I'm surprised you're even up now."

"I need to talk to Ethan," I say, trying to keep my eyes open.

"He's on his way," she says softly. "He should be here soon."

"Don't give me anything else to sleep." I fight to keep my eyes open. "I need to be alert."

"Mayson." She puts her hand into mine, and the heat seeps into my bones. "We got you."

"I still need to be alert," I tell her, not adding that as soon as I'm able to walk, I'm leaving. There is no way I'm going to have this come to their front doors.

Ethan and his family have accepted me and welcomed me with open arms, none of them asking me a single fucking question. Ethan knows what it's like to keep secrets. When he was serving with me, he was hiding and fighting his own secrets. If I'm honest, half the men out there are fighting their own secrets. I lift the cover and see the bandage on my side and see the little bit of pink from the blood. "You got twenty stitches there," she says, and I look at her. My eyes going to the white medical tape on both sides of my ribs. "I can't say for sure without an X-ray, but you have at least three broken ribs."

"I'll survive," I say, my hand holding one side and then the other. "What about my legs?"

"Seventy stitches. So far, they look good. But I'm not a plastic surgeon, so they might leave a scar," she says, and I look down at my hands. They are swollen and red with white bandages around both wrists. "How long were you tied up for?"

I take a deep breath, the pain making me close my eyes. "If you don't mind..."

"If I don't mind," she says, her voice tight. "I do mind." She looks at me, and I see her eyes get a deep blue now. "I mind that for the last fourteen days, I've prayed more than I have in my whole life. If you had died," she says, and I can see that her lower lip quivers just a bit, but she fights it back. "That would have been on my hands. In my house."

"Trust me, if I died, it would not have been at your hands." I put my head back on the pillows propping me up. The feeling of my throbbing head makes me wince.

"What hurts?" she asks, and I know that even though she is pissed, she is still doing her job.

"Head aches," I say, and she walks over to the other side of the room where she had mediation set up. She grabs two pills and brings them over to me.

"I don't want to take anything." I shake my head.

"It's just ibuprofen." She hands them to me, and my hand turns around as she drops them down in the center of my palm. Most of my palms are filled with little cuts from dragging my sorry ass through the forest. "You need to take little sips of water," she says, holding up the cup with the white straw. "If you gulp and drink too much, you'll make yourself sick."

I don't tell her that I know all of this. I don't say anything because what can I say to her? She put her life on the line when she opened that fucking door. When I hear the door open and then slam shut, I'm already ready to get out of bed and throw her out of harm's way. My breathing starts to come in pants, and I start to get up when she puts her hand on my forearm.

"It's Ethan," she says, her voice soft as I look up. "It's just Ethan." Her eyes go a soft blue now, and she repeats herself. "It's just Ethan."

"Well, look at this son of a bitch," Ethan says, coming into the room with his hands on his hips.

"I'm sorry," I tell him, my voice lowering. "I'm so fucking sorry I brought this to your house." I swallow down the lump in my throat. "I just didn't know where else to go."

"Hey," he says, coming to stand beside Chelsea. "You're family," he says. "Where else would you have gone?"

"Fuck if I know." I shake my head, and I know I'm going to have to tell him everything.

"The guys are coming just for a debrief," he tells me, and I nod at him. "Did you have something to eat?"

"He just woke up," Chelsea says to him, and her irritated voice is back. She looks over at me now, and a softer side comes out, "But I can get you some broth." She looks at us and walks out of the room.

I wait for her to be out of ear shot, before turning to him. "The minute I can walk out of here or walk without bleeding, I'm going to be a memory."

"Where will you go?" he asks, and I want to say the cabin.

"Cabin was torched and burned to the ground," he tells

me, and my heart sinks and breaks. That cabin was the only thing I had that was mine. The only thing I decided to keep. The only thing I ever held on to, and now it is gone. I knew I had stayed too long in one place and should have moved along, but the cabin brought me peace. It brought me hope that one day I would be able to live without looking over my shoulder. "Firefighters are saying that it was arson. It was empty." He answers the question I was silently asking myself.

"It was just a house." I say the words. "It can be rebuilt." I don't tell him that I'm not rebuilding it. I'll sell the land, and someone else can put down their own roots.

"Material things can be replaced," he says. "The main thing is you are alive."

"I'm alive," I say. The front door is opened and then closed. The sound of boots clicking on the floor tells me the men of the family have arrived.

They stick together all the time, and when you mess with one, you mess with all of them. I watch them walk into the room. Ethan nods at me silently while Jacob, Casey, Quinn, and Beau come in. The three of them stand side by side.

"You look good," Beau says, and I laugh.

"You always had a way with words." Jacob pushes him.

"What am I supposed to tell him?" Beau looks at Jacob and then Ethan. "You look like death."

"I feel like death," I interrupt them. My leg starts to move out of nerves, and my stomach gets a burning sensation. It rises from my stomach to my chest and then my throat.

"There are so many things to say," I start, my finger tapping the bed. The monitors spike from the way my heart is beating faster and faster.

My mouth is suddenly dry as Ethan talks. "Just start at the beginning," he says, and I look down, gathering all the courage I have. "I don't even know where to start," I say, looking at all of them.

35

"Why don't you answer the biggest question that we have for you?" Jacob says. "Who did this to you? Who would try to kill you?"

Looking each of them square in the eye, I answer them. "My father."

Seven

MAYSON

I watch the eyes of every single man standing in this room. Jacob, Beau, Casey, Ethan, and Quinn. Five men who stand together, regardless of their differences. Five men who at any time would die for their family. Five men who accepted me with no questions asked. "My father."

I don't see her in the room when I talk, but the minute the words leave my lips, she gasps out in shock. My eyes fly to hers, and she can't mask the tears that well in her eyes. She can't even stop the tray in her hand from shaking, and it takes one step from Quinn to grab it before it falls to the floor. "Chelsea," Beau says, coming forward and whispering something in her ear.

She just looks at him and nods her head, turning to walk out of the room, but right before she does, she takes one look over her shoulder at me, and instead of looking at her dead in the eye, I do the coward thing and look down.

My heart beats in my chest, and I'm going to ignore that it's for her. Instead, I'm going to pretend it's because, in a matter of ten minutes, these men who I look up to are going

37

to know all my secrets. I'm going to lie bare to them and hope they still look at me with respect.

I watch Beau walk out of the room with her, and Quinn puts the tray down on the table beside the bed. "I take it you aren't hungry." He smirks at me as I just look down, waiting for Beau to come back.

"Not now, I'm not," I answer, and I want to get up while I have this talk, but I know I can't move. I look at the men in the room and see all the questions written on their faces. Questions I'll have no choice but to answer. Beau walks in with his head down. "She okay?" I shouldn't care, but I do.

"She's just shaken up a bit," he answers honestly. "I don't think she was expecting that answer."

"I mean, why would she?" I laugh nervously.

"Can we get the show going?" Ethan now says with his hands in his back pockets as he looks at me.

"I grew up on the wrong side of the tracks in a single-wide trailer that had seen better days." I start as far back as I can remember. "My mother tried her best to make it as clean as she could, but it was a losing battle even from the beginning." The busted windows held together by a garbage bag and duct tape. That used to have to be replaced every few days because the wind would rip it apart.

"I knew how we lived was wrong, but at seven, all you know is what is presented to you." The memories start to come back as if I've opened a box that has been sealed. "I don't think I ever saw my mother without a bruise on her face or her arms." I swallow now, not sure this was such a good idea. "She hid it as much as she could. Made sure she didn't have any friends she had to explain herself to." I hear one of the men hiss, but I don't stop. "He was always drunk. Under stress." I laugh. "That is what she used to tell me as if it was an excuse to beat your wife. Every single time, she would try to do whatever she had to do to keep him happy.

Regardless of the hell that she was living. She made sure she showed me whatever love she could." I shake my head. "Every fucking Sunday, she would dress up in her only fucking dress. Pack on a pound of makeup and take us to church. I never fucking understood it. We would go to this place, and he would give us stories of hope and happiness." I shake my head. "It was the opposite of how we lived." Closing my eyes for a second, I see her smiling at me. "If I think about it now, she was probably praying for an escape." I look up now, blinking the tears away. "She got her answer when I turned fifteen and she was diagnosed with breast cancer. Of course, we were in the hospital because my father had busted her head open with a frying pan." I don't tell them he did that because she ran out of food to cook him because he had taken his last paycheck and used it to get drunk and then fuck a hooker.

I close my eyes and can see her in front of me as if it was yesterday, sitting in the middle of the bed. Her body almost a skeleton as she tried to fight "They didn't catch it fast enough, and in three weeks, it had taken over her whole body." The lump in my throat is as big as a boulder. "It took three weeks for her to get diagnosed and to pass away."

I look at the men now as they stand there. Quinn shows on his face the anguish that I felt all those years ago. "My father didn't even claim her body."

"Motherfucker," Jacob says, shaking his head and looking down at his feet. Beau hisses out now. Casey and Ethan stand there with nothing on their faces. Both of them are trained not to show emotion.

"So they buried her in an unmarked grave," I tell them. "Now with my mother gone, there was nowhere he could get rid of 'his stress.'" I use air quotes. "It started slowly at first." I see his face in my head. "A punch in the ribs. A kick in the back when I was walking away. A backhand slap when I didn't look up at him. A punch in the head when I looked up at him too long."

I see that Quinn is crouched down with his back against the wall and his hands in front of his mouth.

"When I was sixteen, I ended up in the hospital with a broken arm in two places." I look down at the scar that is now covered with my ink. "They knew I didn't trip on anything, but at that point, what were they going to do? Get CPS involved when I was close to being an adult."

"They could have helped you," Beau says, and Ethan laughs.

"You think they are going to help a sixteen-year-old boy?" Ethan shakes his head and looks over to me. "Nothing they could have done would have helped."

"So I kept my head down. I made friends with the janitor at the school, and he would allow me to stay with him while he cleaned the school. I would hit the gym while he cleaned. I stayed there until it was dark out, then snuck in when I knew he would be passed out in the single recliner."

"How big did you get?" Casey asks me.

"I went from a scrawny one-hundred-and-ten-pound, five-foot-six boy to a six-foot-two, one-hundred-and-sixty-pound man," I tell him. "It happened so fast that I don't think he was expecting it. Doesn't mean he didn't try to push me around. He did."

"It must have been harder for him," Jacob says with a smile on his face.

"It was, but that doesn't mean he didn't try," I say, swallowing. "He broke my leg with a metal pipe when I was sleeping." I look at Quinn, who hasn't moved since I started my story. "I should have known it was coming. It took over six months to heal because"—I look down—"I couldn't go to the hospital."

"What?" Quinn asks me.

"I was almost eighteen. It was going to make another case, and I didn't want it. I had made a plan by that point, and I just needed to be on alert every single day." I swallow. "So every single day, I got just a touch stronger. Every single day, I waited. Every single day, I also wondered if it would be my last." I look down at my hand. "He was becoming more unhinged as the days went on. He lost his job, and the money was not coming in. I don't know what he was doing at the end, and I can only imagine how low he must have gotten. But I didn't care because it would be only a matter of time until I would be gone."

"What happened next?" Beau asks me, his jaw tight as he bounces on his heels.

"He came home loaded and drunk," I say as the last day comes back like a movie playing over and over again. "Walked in or actually stumbled in." If I close my eyes, I can still smell him faintly. "Tried to turn on the lights, and they had been cut. I was sitting down in the dark trailer with just a little candle lit." I swallow now. "The rain had just started very much like two weeks ago. I sat watching him toss things around in frustration that he couldn't control the situation. I remember the sound of the rain hitting the tin roof, the pitter-patter of it, and the light from the lightning coming into the trailer. I knew the minute he looked at me that it was going to be that night. I knew that it was no turning back. He came toward me, calling me every single name in the book. He couldn't even speak. All his words were slurred. I was no good for nothing. The biggest mistake of his life. It wasn't the first time he'd told me that, and unlike when I was thirteen, I didn't shut my mouth on this day." I smile as the tears roll down my face. "I gave it right back to him. He was a spineless piece of shit." Casey smiles with me. "He was not a man. A man takes care of his family." I look at the men who actually do everything that I've just said. "He did not like that!"

"I can imagine," Jacob says, and I swear I see his chest puff out proud.

"I got up then to stand in front of him." Another tear comes, and I just let it drop onto the covers. "I don't think he realized I was a little taller than him at this point. He pushed my shoulder. I remember telling myself to let it be. I was going to just take my shit and go, but then he looked me in the eye and told me that I should have died with that piece-of-shit woman he got stuck with." My eyes fly to Quinn, who has his own tears running down his face. "I struck him for the first time in my life. Punched him straight in the face. He stumbled back and then touched his jaw, turning to spit blood out of his mouth. He sneered at me, and I knew he was high. Instead of walking away, he walked toward me again. This time, I swung with everything I had. My fist connected with his jaw at the same time as the thunder rolled in. He stumbled back, falling over his ratty recliner, and instead of just grabbing my bag and walking out, I went to him. Hitting him over and over again, I knew in that single trailer where I grew up, I knew only one of us was walking out alive, and the other person would be left to die. I hit him until my hand was broken." Looking down at the hand, I open and close it. "I left thinking he was dead." I look at them. "The next day, Mayson Carey was born, and Braxton Michaels was dead."

Eight

CHELSEA

"The next day, Mayson Carey was born, and Braxton Michaels was dead." I put my hand against the wall as my knees give out on me. The tears are flowing like a river down my face. I can't imagine what it must be like. "I thought he was dead." I put my hand to my mouth in order to stop the sob that wants to rip through me. "Left him for dead, and then I joined the military. Never," he says, his voice going down. "Never did I think he was alive."

"Did you check his pulse?" Ethan asks him.

"No," he says. "There was no way I thought he could survive."

"He found you," Quinn says, and I stop breathing as I hear him answer.

"Might as well get Chelsea," Mayson says. "She saved me from dying, so she should hear how it happened."

I get up slowly and walk to the kitchen to grab a glass. Turning around, I head straight to the cabinet where I keep my grandfather's special drink. I untwist the top and pour two fingers in the glass. Ethan walks in at the same time as I pick the glass up and take down the gulp.

The burning makes me cough, and I put the back of my hand in front of my mouth. "Did you hear?" Ethan says, looking at me, and I just look back at him.

"You can't leave him here," I tell him, and he just looks at me. "I'm not kidding, Ethan. You can not keep him here."

"Because of his past?" He glares at me, and I glare back at him.

"You fucking know what that man just dished out." I point toward the hallway, ignoring the tears rolling down my face. "What he just put out in that room. He needs help." I put my hand to my chest as his words play over and over in my head. I can't save him is the only thing I can tell myself.

"He needs you," he says. "Look at what you did for him so far. You don't have to do anything else but make sure he stays alive," Ethan says, and we both stop talking when we see Quinn standing there.

"She heard?" he mentions with his chin toward me, and Ethan nods. "Something tells me that what is coming next is going to hurt even more."

"Let's go find out," I say, pouring another shot and then taking it and coughing again.

"How many is that?" Ethan asks me.

"Not enough that I can still hear his broken voice in my head," I say and walk into the room.

I look over at my father, who is about to step forward to come to me, but I give him a silent shake of my head, and he stops. My eyes fly toward Mayson, and I move them away, seeing that they are red. I want to ask him all the questions. I want him to know it doesn't matter what happened. He's still himself.

"Well," I say, looking at him now, putting my hands in front of me. "What are we talking about?"

"You can stop pretending you didn't hear everything before," Mayson says, and I look at him.

"You're in my house, and the walls are not soundproof." I look over at my uncle Casey. "So yeah, I heard."

"Good," Mayson says. "Saves me time to rehash it." He tries to sit up, but he winces. The day after he got here, Casey showed up with a hospital bed. I was shocked that in thirty minutes, my old bed was out, and the hospital bed was in. To be honest, it was more convenient for me.

I walk over to the side table and grab his glass of water and hand it to him. "This will help." He nods at me and takes a couple of sips.

"I joined the military as Mayson." He continues his story. "Every single day, I was petrified they would find out what I did. Every single time I got summoned, I thought this is it. I'm going to jail for murder." He smirks now. "But nothing. No one knew or found out. I made sure I never got a credit card. I paid for everything in cash. Stayed in a motel to avoid getting an apartment so they wouldn't do a background check. I went back to the trailer park and found that the whole park had been wiped out. Turns out, that night a tornado had come through and wrecked everything."

"Did you check for a death certificate?" Uncle Casey asks him, and he shakes his head. He takes the phone out of his pocket typing something into it.

"I had just come back from my last tour. Three weeks ago, I guess. I walked into the cabin and knew right away something wasn't right. Felt it in my stomach and the hairs on the back of my neck stood up." He looks down as his hands start to shake. "For the past eight years, I've been leaving things in a certain way to make sure no one surprised me." He looks at Ethan, faking laughing. "Must be the training." Ethan laughs with him. "He swung the bat before I was able to grab the gun," he says. "Knocked me out."

"How long?" Ethan asks him, and he looks down.

"Long enough to drag me out behind the cabin," he says, looking at him, "and tie me to a tree."

"Wait a second," I say, stepping forward, and he stops talking. My heart speeds up as I think about him locked up, not only for an hour but a week. "Are you telling me that you were locked up for a whole week?"

"Five days," he corrects me.

"It's fine," he tells me, looking me in the eyes. He tries to smile at me, but it's a sad fucking smile. "He tied me to the tree, and every day, he would come out and knock me around." Quinn hisses, and I look over at him, and he shakes his head and holds his neck in his hand. "Three," he says the number. "Always three knocks in a row."

"This is insane." The words come out of my mouth.

"Chelsea," my father says my name. "Let him finish."

I shake my head and put my hand to my stomach. "He stabbed me six times but got the same one twice." I shake my head, trying to block out the words. "He dropped the knife one night and forgot about it."

"Was this before or after you were shot?" I ask him, looking over at the men in the room and wondering why the fuck they haven't said shit to him.

"Same day," he says. "He did my legs first, and then when he dropped the knife, he took the gun out."

"For fuck's sake," Ethan says now, and I want him to get angry. I want him to ask all the fucking questions.

"I got the knife and hid it. But not before he came out and hit me some more," he says, and I look at him.

"I've seen your wounds," I say. "There is no way that was done with a hand."

"You're right," he says, looking straight at me. "Sometimes, they were his steel-toed boots. Other times, it was the bat just for good measure," he says. "I got loose and waited or maybe I passed out, but I knew the lay of the land." He looks at Ethan. "I know the surroundings like I know the back of my hand. I waited until I knew he passed out and then crawled." He sits up now as proud as can be, this man who just spent five days being tortured by the person who should have protected him. "I don't know if you can call it crawling." I look down at his hands. "I pulled myself inch by fucking inch," he says, and my stomach starts to turn. "It took me over eight hours to get to my neighbor's land, which takes thirty minutes to hike." My head spins around and around as he says the next part. "There was no way he would have left me alive. Not this time."

"It was your training," my uncle Jacob says. "Your training saved you."

"I don't know what the fuck it was, but at one point, I just wanted to let fucking go. I could barely fucking see out of one eye. Every single time I took a breath, it felt like I was being stabbed over and over again. Every time I moved, I felt the stab wounds in my legs rip open even more. Forget about the bullet wound. Forget about the gash in my head or the fact that one of my eyes was swollen shut," he says. "I got to the truck, and the only place I could think of was making it here. For five days, he beat me and tortured me. He wanted me to beg for my life." The words pour out of him so painfully. "He wanted me to beg him and bow down to him. The more I fought it, the harder the hits came, but there was no fucking way in hell I would bend to him. There was no fucking way I was going to let him win." He shakes his head, and now the tears roll out of me over and over again. "I was not going to let him fucking win!" he roars out. "Not then and not fucking now. If I was going to die, I was going to die on my terms." I turn now, walking out of the room straight to the bathroom.

"Chelsea." I hear my father calling my name, but I close the door and make it just in time to throw up in the toilet. "Honey," he says softly, and I get up, walking over to the sink. Turning on the tap, I cup my hands under the stream. I wash my face, then open the bathroom door just a touch, seeing my father standing there with worry all over his face. I push open the door, letting my father come in. "Honey." He whispers my nickname and holds out his arms, and I run into him, my sob muffled in his chest.

His arms go around me, and I know that I'm safe. I know he has me for as long as I need him. "It's okay," he whispers in my ear.

"His father did that to him," I say, my eyes open and are focused on the wall. "Beat him to an inch of his life." I let go of him now. "How? How can someone do that to their own child?"

"I can't explain that to you," he says. "I mean, my father was no walk in the park, and he definitely never helped me with homework." He has never really spoken about his father. He was dead before I was born. I do know from the stories that people tell me, that he was not a nice man. He was the reason that Ethan left us when he turned twenty-one.

"That man is lucky to be alive," I say softly. "You didn't see the wounds, Dad," I say softly. "You didn't spend over six hours stitching him up. You didn't have to fix a man whose own father did that to him."

"I didn't." He leans now against the doorjamb of the bathroom, putting his hands in his pockets.

"Now that you know what he's up against, you still want him gone?" I hear Ethan say from behind my father.

"What if his father finds him here?" I ask him and then look at my father. "Are you going to be okay with me being a sitting duck until his father comes back and finishes the job?"

"He won't get close enough," my uncle Casey says from behind Ethan. "I would never put you in harm's way." I shake my head, not listening to what he has to say. "I promise you that."

I look at my father, then to Uncle Casey, who just smiles shyly at me, and then to Ethan. "Fine," I say, not believing I'm going to say these words. The thought of letting my family down is too much for me to handle. "He can stay."

Nine

MAYSON

I watch her run away from the room, and I have to look down at my arm, blinking away the tears that will come for her. Her face was riddled with tears as I told them how my own father tied me to a fucking tree for five days and tortured me. I take a deep breath, the pain a little less than it was yesterday but barely. "She going to be okay?" I ask, looking up to see Jacob and Quinn left in the room.

"Not a chance," Quinn says at the same time that Jacob says, "She'll be fine."

I laugh at both of them. "Well, that sounds convincing."

"It was a hard story," Jacob says, looking at me. "For anyone to hear."

"I can imagine, especially with the way this family was brought up." I look at them both, and I'm going to admit that I envy what they have. It's what you read about in story books, and then to see that it actually exists, it's a gift.

"I want you to know," Jacob says, coming toward the bed. "That we are going to stand by you."

I nod my head, not sure I can say anything when Ethan

and Casey come back into the room. "Sorry about that," Ethan says, and I look at Casey.

"Is she okay?" I ask, knowing that this is too much for her. It's too much for me, and I lived through it. It also kills me that I brought this to her front door, and she got involved with this.

"Beau is with her," Casey says to me, and a second later, they both come back into the room.

"Chelsea," I say her name, and she just looks at me, and the redness of her eyes stabs me in the heart. There is so much I want to say to her, but here in the middle of her family is not the place, so I say the only thing that comes to mind. "I'm sorry." I leave out what I'm sorry for.

"Okay, so now that we have some answers," Casey says, and her eyes never leave mine. "I'll fill you in on what I found."

Chelsea now looks over at him. "The car was reported stolen."

"I called Mr. Harvey," Ethan says to the room. "Told him you had an emergency and your car didn't work."

I shake my head. "He is never going to believe that."

"He didn't," Ethan laughs, "but he said to tell that son of a bitch he better put gas in the tank."

I laugh now; we didn't always get along, but we did share a couple of moments where we respected each other. He's a veteran and fought in the Vietnam War, so we bonded over surviving and serviving. "I'm sure he did."

"I got a copy of the fire report," Casey says. "Arson."

"Wait, what?" Chelsea asks, looking around at all the men in the room and then looking down.

"I'm already in this," she says. "So if you guys want to suddenly protect me, should you have not brought him to my house?"

"She's right," I say to the room. "She deserves to know what we know." I look at her and see her beauty, and then I tell myself to back off. She is too young for me, and besides, she doesn't need someone who has nothing.

"Fine," Ethan says. "The cabin was burned to the ground."

"Did you find his father in there?" she asks, hopeful that this is all over.

"No," Casey says. "And." He looks down. "Your gun is missing also."

"Of course it is," Chelsea says. "How do you think he got shot?"

"We have eyes everywhere," Casey says. "We have this house wired up tight."

"We can take shifts," Quinn says.

"Why?" Chelsea asks, and we all look at her. "If no one knows he's here, why would everyone be here? We need to act as normal as we can. So it's suspicious if Quinn is spending the night or Ethan isn't home with Emily at night."

"She's right," I say, looking at her. "During the day, people can come and go. But the night has to be normal."

"I'm not leaving her all night alone," Beau says, shaking his head. "No fucking way. No offense, Mayson, but..."

"I would do the same," I agree with him.

"Um, I think I can stick up for myself," Chelsea says. "As long as I have my gun, I'll be okay."

"You can't be serious," Quinn says, looking around. "This man is unhinged. He almost killed his own son. It is going to take nothing for him to off Chelsea."

"I would never let anything hurt her," I say, looking straight at her.

"And how do you think you will protect her?" Quinn says, almost shouting.

"Son," Casey says to him, and he just shakes his head.

"No, Dad," he says. "Answer me?" His eyes come to me. "How are you going to protect her? You can't even stand."

"We will have eyes on the house all day and night long. We just won't have someone in here."

"What's the fastest we can get here?" Jacob looks over at Casey.

"Seventeen seconds," he answers, and even my mouth hangs open. "We have someone in the barn at all times watching."

"My horse is in there," Chelsea says, and Quinn smirks. "Where is Bella?"

"She didn't like the extra people in there," Quinn says, "and she got a little testy."

"How so?" Chelsea asks, folding her arms over her chest.

"She tried to kick Diego when he tried to give her water." Quinn laughs.

"Okay, is there anything else we need to talk about?" I ask. "The pain level is going higher and higher." Chelsea looks at the monitor. "I'm fine."

"He needs rest," Chelsea says, looking at the guys. Casey and Quinn leave together and so do Beau and Jacob. Beau gives Chelsea a big hug and whispers something in her ear. She nods at him as he turns and nods his head my way.

Ethan is the last one to leave the room. "I'll get him something to drink," Chelsea says and turns to walk out of the room.

We both wait until she is gone before we look at each other. "I'm leaving," I tell him, and he just looks at me. "The minute that I can."

"You think I don't know that?" he says, putting his hands over his chest.

"I'm going to find him," I tell him as the rage fills my veins now. "I'm going to fucking find him, and when I do, I'm going to kill him." I smile now. "I'm going to catch him when he least expects it. Wound him and then." I smile so big it hurts my face. "I'm going to look him straight in the eyes when

53

I put a bullet between those eyes. The last thing that mother-fucker is going to see is me." I swallow. "Piece by fucking piece. I'm going to take from him."

"I'll be ready when you are," he says, and I just look at him. A lump in my throat stops me from snapping back at him. I shake my head, looking down at the bandages around my wrists.

"No, you won't," I say, my eyes staying down. "You aren't getting close to this. Think about your family." I look straight at him.

"I am." He looks me straight in the eye. "You're my brother. You would do the same for me without thinking twice."

"Yeah, because I have nothing to lose," I tell him. "Nothing. You have a wife. You have children. Go home, Ethan," I tell him, and he just looks at me.

"I'll call you later," he says, not arguing with me, and I know it's because he can feel that I'm exhausted.

Mentally and physically exhausted, I close my eyes and lie back on the pillow. I hear her feet coming closer and closer to the room. I open my eyes while she walks in. "Do you want to have something to drink?" she asks me, and I look at her. I've watched her from afar for the past seven years. Since I first met her, she has never backed down from a challenge. I would watch her laugh with her cousins. Spar with Quinn. Bake with her grandmother and then bask in love from her grandfather. "How are you feeling?" she says, stopping beside my bed and holding out the glass of water for me.

"Like I've been shot and stabbed," I tell her, and she looks down at my hands. "But I'll survive."

"I'm going to clean the dressing of your gunshot wound." She turns, grabbing the stainless steel bowl. She walks to the bathroom and fills it with water. She comes back, placing it on the bed beside me. I watch her hands as she lifts the white gauze and finally sees the bullet wound.

"It looks pretty," I say, looking down as she washes the wound with the warm water.

"It looks horrible," she says. "It's turning purple all around." She takes her finger and traces the color. "If it starts spreading, it might be an infection."

"I'm sure it's fine," I say to her as she puts Vaseline on the wound and then places another bandage on it.

"There," she says, going back into the bathroom and turning on the water again. I close my eyes, ignoring the stinging that is going right through me now.

I feel the covers come off me and look down at my legs. Five big white bandages all down my legs. Three on one leg, two on the other. Both on the upper thigh. A mistake for him right there, you always break at least one foot, both if you really want to fuck them up. I'll teach him that the next time I see him.

"What are you thinking of right there?" Chelsea says, looking at me and the ECG machine. "Your heart rate just spiked there. Is it too much to see your wounds?" I see her hands shake a bit, but she covers it up fast.

"No," I tell her. "To be honest, the stab wounds aren't the worst I've been hurt." Her eyes fly up to see mine. The questions are written all over her face. "Is that why your heartbeat went up? Were you thinking about it?"

"No, actually," I answer her and figure that there is nothing in this world that can happen between us. Nothing on this earth could ever make her look at me like I'm not from a monster. "I was thinking that my father was stupid for just stabbing me in the thighs." Her hand stops moving, she looks up at me again. "He should have broken my foot." She looks down at the wounds. "So I couldn't walk."

She doesn't say anything to me; instead, she finishes

cleaning me up. "All done," she says as she finishes my last wound. She walks over to the desk and brings me back two pills. "This should help with the pain."

"I'm good," I tell her. "I don't want to be loopy."

"Your body needs to rest to heal," she says, and I take the two pills and then take three sips of water. "I'll be back," she says, leaving the room, and my eyes close the second she is out of sight, and the darkness takes over.

"You can't run from me for long." I hear my father's voice. "I found you once, I'll find you again."

My eyes open, and I gasp out, my chest rising and falling so fast I can't catch my breath. My blurry eyes roam the dark room. My eyes go to the window, and I see two eyes looking back at me before the crashing of glass fills the room.

Ten

CHELSEA

The sound of glass makes me jump out of bed. The only thing I grab is the gun on my bedside table as I run out of the room and toward the sound of groaning. My palms are sweaty, and my heart is beating so fast I can't even breathe properly. As I run in the darkness, so many things rush at me.

I run into the room, the darkness all around me as I step on the glass. The burning is going straight from my foot to my calf. I ignore the pain as I turn on the light, my gun still pointed. "Fuck," I hear hissed from the floor and look down to see Mayson lying on his stomach. One of the lamps from the side table on the floor is smashed, the glass of water smashed into little pieces.

My eyes fly to the window, seeing it's still closed as I look back down at Mayson. Blood all around him, I rush to him, putting the gun down beside me as I turn him over to his back. "Mayson," I whisper, and his eyes open. The anguish and pain is written all over his face. "You're bleeding," I tell him, looking down at the blood that seeped through the white shirt he is wearing. "I need to get you up," I say and turn around to

57

pick him up by his shoulders. I slip my hands under his arms, and he fights with me.

"I got it," he hisses out angrily. I look at him as he struggles to get up and into the bed. I walk over to him to help him get his legs into the bed, but his voice angrily stops me. "I said I got it." He doesn't look at me as he gets back into bed.

I look at him, my heart thumping so fast in my chest that the heat is creeping up the back of my neck. The sweat beads all over his forehead, making me know he's taken more energy getting into bed than he cares to admit. His chest is rising and falling as my eyes go to the drop of blood leaking down his side and onto the white pad under him.

"I have to get the bleeding to stop," I say, turning to walk away and wincing. I stop mid-step and look down to see blood coming out of the bottom of my foot. "Shit," I hiss out, looking over my shoulder to see his eyes looking straight at my foot.

"Make sure there isn't glass stuck in there." He motions with his chin toward my foot. I just turn my head back, making my way to the bathroom, putting the pressure on the heel of my foot.

I walk over to the bathtub and sit on the edge. Turning on the water, I wait until it's warm before I let it wash over my foot. The heat stings just a bit. Taking a second for myself, I close my eyes and let my heart calm down. So many fucking things were going through my head when I heard the glass crashing. I thought it was his father. I thought I would walk into the room and find him dead. "Are you okay in there?" I hear his voice and wipe away the lone tear rolling down my cheek.

"Yeah," I say, grabbing a towel to wrap my foot in it, trying to close off my head. I apply pressure to it and then unwrap it and see it is sliced right through. "It went right through!" I shout, looking down at the red line straight down the bottom of my foot. Little droplets of blood are starting to come out.

"Do you need stitches?" he shouts, and I take a look at it.

"I think I'll just need to bandage it," I tell him, wrapping the towel around it and applying pressure, hoping to stop the bleeding. Swinging my feet out of the tub, I get up, placing all the pressure on the heel of my foot as I walk back into the room. "I need shoes," I say to him, avoiding his eyes. I slip my feet into my surgical Crocs.

I close my eyes and swallow down the lump in my throat. Taking a deep breath, I go back into the room. "Okay." I look at him, stopping in my tracks. His shirt is already off, and he is taking off his own bandage. "What do we have there?" I say once I'm beside his bed, looking down to see that the stitches are still there but not sure they are all there.

"Nothing," he says. "I'm fine."

"Let me clean it and make sure you didn't pop a stitch," I say, walking over to the bathroom. The sting of my foot hits me, and I know I should check it out and make sure it doesn't get infected. He lets me clean it without saying anything to me. His head lies back on the pillows, and his eyes close. After I clean the blood off, I see he isn't bleeding anymore. "All stitches accounted for." I smile, but he doesn't look at me. "Must have just irritated them when you fell off the bed," I say, and he just nods his head. "Why didn't you call me?" I look at him, and he shakes his head.

"It was nothing," he tells me, his voice tight. I look over at him, and I know he's lying. I know that it was something. I see the fear in his eyes as he looks at me and then back out the window.

"I don't think you ending up face-first on the floor is nothing," I tell him, turning and walking back into the hall closet to grab a broom. I walk back into the room, ignoring his eyes on me. "Should I call Ethan?" I ask, not looking at him as I sweep up the broken glass.

"I'm fine," he says. "I'll pay you back for the lamp," he says, and I laugh out bitterly now.

"I don't want your money," I tell him, turning and walking to the kitchen and dumping the broken glass into the garbage. I put the broom away and walk back to the bedroom. I find him with his head back on the pillows as he looks up at the ceiling. "Do you need anything else?" I ask him and he turns his face to look at me. The fear is all over it.

"What the hell were you thinking?" he says, and I just look at him confused.

"I'm sorry?" I say. Obviously, I've misheard him. Surely, he's not coming at me with this attitude.

"Running in here like a bat out of hell." His eyes fly to mine. "Without thinking twice about it. Coming in here half naked." His words cut me to the core.

I stand straight now, looking at him as he stares at me with his eyes dead. There is nothing in them anymore. It's like a switch went out in them. "I was sleeping after being awoken and scared shitless," I tell him, trying to keep my calm instead of really showing him what a bat out of hell looks like. A draft of cold air runs through me, and I can feel the goose bumps all over my bare arms and legs. "When you decided you were too macho to ask for help when you tried to grab a glass of water." His eyes never leave mine. "So excuse me for not grabbing my robe on my way here." I advance on him one more step. "The only thing that went through my head was getting to you in case..."

"In case what?" he says, his voice soft. "In case my father came and finished the job?" He laughs.

I shake my head. "I'm not going to be the one you take your shit out on." My calm leaving me like the air leaves a balloon. "I've bent over fucking backward for you. I've done shit that I was not comfortable with, and I did them for you." I point at him. "So spin that while you're on your high horse," I say, turning and walking out of the room. Not even caring anymore. I walk to my room and slam the door behind me just to show him. "Asshole."

I walk to my bathroom, kicking off my shoe and seeing the towel soaked in blood. "Shit," I hiss out, walking over to grab the first aid kit from the drawer. The anger in me is making me ignore the pain shooting through me.

My mind replays the scene as I grab the glue. Once I glue the cut back together, I place a bandage on it. Washing off my hands, I walk out of the bathroom, not putting all my pressure on my foot.

I walk toward the bed and then turn suddenly, going to check on him. I try not to make any noise. The hallway is dark, and when I get closer to his bedroom, I see the light is off also. I stand here at the doorway, looking in at him.

His head turns, looking in my direction. "I'm sorry, Chelsea," he says softly and doesn't wait for me to say anything. Instead, he turns his head toward the window. "Good night."

"Good night," I say, turning and walking back to my room. I slip into bed, turning on my side and I watch the darkness become light before my eyes slip closed.

When I wake up the next morning, my bedroom door is closed, and I panic that I missed something. I grab my robe and walk out of the room, but the stinging of my foot makes me stop as Ethan walks out of Mayson's room.

"Is there a reason your gun is in his room?" He puts his arms over his chest. "Actually," he says, "maybe you should tell me why you didn't call me before you went running into his room."

I glare at him. "Which question do you want answered

first?" I fold my hands over my chest, and now he glares back at me.

He doesn't say anything as he looks at me , "What happened to your foot?"

"That's three questions," I tell him, "and I need coffee." I ignore him and hobble over to the coffee machine. I look over and see that it's already noon. "What time did you get here?"

"Eight," he says. "You were passed out snoring, so I closed your door."

"I didn't hear you." I grab the cup of coffee and bring it to my lips.

"So let's hear it," he says, ignoring what I just said.

"What is there to say? I heard crashing in the middle of the night, and when I ran to make sure he was okay, I sliced my foot." I hobble over to one of the stools.

"From what Mayson said..." he says, and I pfft out.

"From what Mayson said what?" I ask him. "If you don't like it, take him and leave." He just looks at me. "If I'm doing something you don't approve of, you are more than welcome to take him and bring him to your house." I ignore the pounding in my chest and the burning in my stomach, thinking of him being anywhere else without me being able to make sure he is okay. "But if you are going to leave him here, you are going to do it with my rules."

"And what are those?" He leans back on the counter, crossing his feet at his ankles.

"One, what I do and when I do it, shouldn't be questioned," I say. "I am not going to tiptoe around. This is my house. I did what needed to be done at the moment."

"You could have been hurt," he points out.

"And he could have been dead," I counter at him. "But I'm not, and neither is he."

"But you're hurt," he says, and I roll my eyes.

"It's a cut," I tell him, not even going to mention I had to glue the cut back together.

"You should have called," he tells me.

"What would you have done?" I ask and don't give him a chance to say anything else. "Raced over here for nothing. If there was any danger, they would have seen it." I mention the cameras. "Now, if you'll excuse me," I say, getting up. "I have been craving biscuits and gravy." I walk back toward my bedroom, ignoring the pull to check on him.

Eleven

MAYSON

I listen to the conversation taking place in the kitchen as I try to forget about what a dick I was to her last night. She rushed in here to save me, and all I could do was get my pride hurt and yell at her. It wasn't my finest moment, especially since she was standing there bleeding. Instead of burying the anger, I just came at her.

"I have been craving biscuits and gravy," I hear her say and then hear her bedroom door slam again. She seems to be doing that a lot since I got here.

I hear his footsteps coming back toward my bedroom, and when Ethan walks in with his head shaking, I am rolling my lips, trying not to laugh. "Well, looks like you sure took care of that," I tell him, and he just glares at me.

"What got her panties in a twist? Who pissed her off?" Ethan says, looking at me, sitting down in the same chair he did this morning when he walked in. He stood there in the middle of the room and watched me walk back to the bed, never once asking me if I needed help.

When I woke up this morning, my eyes flew around the room, making sure everything was where it should be. I took my time sitting up and trying to breathe through the pain. It was shooting right up my side. I slung my legs out of bed and tried standing up. It took me over an hour to get to the bathroom. My body shook once I got there. I sat on the toilet with my eyes focused on the tub, seeing the spots of dried blood on the side. Anger filled me for so many different reasons. Reasons I don't want to think about.

"You pissed her off," Ethan says, and I just laugh now. His foot goes up and down.

"I might have pissed her off," I agree to that. "But from the sounds of it, you pissed her off by not asking her nicely." I point at him, and I don't say anything else because she comes into the room.

Today, she's wearing black tights with a white shirt that shows off a little of her toned stomach. "Good morning," she says, tying her blond hair on top of her head. I look down and see she has a white bandage around her foot.

"Morning." I smile at her, and she comes in. "How is the foot?" I ask her, and she looks down at it.

"I've had worse injuries," she says, looking at Ethan. "How are the wounds?" She looks at the bandages now. "Any bleeding?"

"No," I say, moving the covers down so she can see the clean bandage.

"Perfect." She looks around. "So today would be a good day to get out of bed." She smiles, and it lights up her whole face. It's carefree and fucking perfect. "Ethan." She looks over at him. "Why don't you help him to the couch, and I might share breakfast with you?" Then she turns to me. "Sorry, no biscuits and gravy for you. It's a liquid diet for the next couple of days."

"It's lunchtime," he tells her, not even getting up to help. "And he can get himself to the couch. He doesn't need anyone to baby him."

"I forgot you guys are big strong men. Shall I go outside and bring in some dirt so you can rub yourself with it?" She points with her thumb over her shoulder.

She walks out of the room, and I look over at Ethan. "How good of a shot is she?"

He gets up from the chair. "Better than me," he tells me, and my eyes open wide. He's one of the best shots I've ever seen in my life. "We did a one-on-one when I got back. Brought out the cans from the barn. Lined them up. Two cans, different areas. First one to turn and shoot wins. She got it in point four seconds." I raise an eye. "Took me point two seconds more." I clap my hands together, laughing at him. "Now get your lazy ass out of bed. Because my sister is making biscuits and gravy and apart from my grandmother's, hers are second best. I will not let you fuck this up for me."

"Roger that," I tell him, and I swing my legs off the bed and put on the shorts he brought me this morning. I put my hands on the bed, getting up slowly, pulling the stitches tight now. I put my hand to my side when I stand straight and hope I didn't pull anything. "I walk as slow as a ninety-five-year-old man."

"We can get you a cane," Ethan jokes with me. "Or you know, those walker things with wheels." He walks beside me just in case I go down.

"Fuck you," I say, lifting my hand and giving him the bird, but everything in my body hurts now.

I hear the soft music playing when I get to the opening of the family room attached to the kitchen. "Is there a blanket somewhere?" I look over at Ethan. "The whole couch is white, and I'm afraid I'll bleed on it."

"In the hallway," Chelsea says, pointing toward a white door. "There are some in there, but it's not necessary. I live here. It's not a museum, so things are bound to get dirty."

I look over at the L-shaped white couch with gray throw

pillows with a black coffee table in the middle. Two big single white couches face the L-shaped couch with a little gray table between them, and she has a vase of tulips on there. I walk over, sitting down, and I'm not going to lie. I let a big sigh out. "Do you want water or juice?" she asks, and I look at her as she kneads the dough with flour on her face as she sings along to the music.

"I'm good for now," I tell her, and she claps her hands, then rubs them together and comes over to me. "Here you go," she says, handing me the black remote. "You can watch television. I'll turn off the music."

"You don't have to do that," I tell her, and I smell her citrus smell. She turns, and I see her use her heel to walk.

"I have to run out," Ethan says, coming back from the back room. "Gabriel just got called into the office. The kid is in the principal's office in pre-school."

"Oh, no," Chelsea says. "Is everything okay?"

"He stuck up for a kid that was being bullied," he says with a smile.

"Then I think he deserves ice cream," Chelsea says, smiling.

Ethan nods and walks out of the house, slamming the door behind him. Instead of turning on the television, I watch Chelsea. "You watching me is weird," she says, cutting the biscuits with the round silver cylinder.

"I didn't know you cooked," I tell her.

"There is a lot about me that you don't know," she counters. "Every single time you've been around me, you have said a total of maybe five words."

She is not wrong. "I'm sure I said more than five words," I tell her, but I know I didn't. Every time I saw her, and she was next to me, my tongue got suddenly heavy and my throat closed up. It was the weirdest thing. I also got a hard-on every single time, and then I had to remind myself that she was six years younger than me, and I was a dirty animal.

"I mean, when you did meet me, you said, 'It's great to meet you. I've heard a lot about you,'" she says, laughing. "I remember because all I kept thinking was who was the hot guy." I swallow now.

"I remember seeing you across the lawn and then thinking how beautiful you were," I tell her. "And then Ethan told me your name, and I just felt like an old creep," I admit to her.

"Oh, wait," she says, turning and putting the tray in the oven. "Once, we did have an in-depth conversation." I look over at her. "Do you not remember? It got pretty heated."

My heart speeds up, and I just shake my head. "There was no way in fuck we had a conversation, and it was heated," I tell her, trying to remember when this happened as I sit on the couch watching her.

"It was, and it was over pizza." She folds her arms over her chest. "It got heated when you didn't get off my ass about pineapples on pizza."

I put my head back and laugh, but the pulling in my side makes me wince. Her face goes white as she looks at me, and I hold up my hand to stop her from coming over. "I remember that. Pineapple is not supposed to be on pizza."

"Yeah, well, we can agree to disagree." She laughs, turning, and I see her take a pan out as she starts the gravy.

"So why did you want to become a nurse?" I ask her, trying to make it less awkward between the two of us.

"Gabriel," she tells me without skipping a beat. She walks to the stainless steel fridge, grabbing stuff in her hands. "The minute he was born, I had this fear that if something happened to him, I wouldn't be able to help him." I watch her talk. "The fear grew, and I just decided to volunteer at the clinic in the next town. Dr. Gabe is a family friend, and he made me shadow him, and I just fell in love with it. Knowing that you are helping someone is just..."

"It's a rush," I tell her, my mouth watering as she whisks something on the stove. My stomach is suddenly rumbling.

"I never thought about it like that." She looks over. "If you weren't in the military, what do you think you would be doing?"

"That's a hard question," I tell her honestly. "I've thought about it, especially when I was on tour. You are stuck with hours and hours of waiting. Your head plays your life over and over." I shrug now. "I never stayed in one place long enough to want to do anything else. I would stay in my cabin and wait for my next deployment. In the end, I think the military saved me."

"Everything happens for a reason," she says, and I see her pouring milk in the pan. "Every single thing has a chain reaction."

"You really believe that?" I ask her. "You think my father shooting and torturing me was for a reason?"

She turns down the stove and turns to look at me. "Yes. You joining the military and going on those tours. You were meant to do that. You save people. You serve and protect. That is your reason." She walks over to the sink and washes her hands. "Just like me being home when you showed up. I was supposed to be home next week," she tells me, and my heart speeds up. "But I come home early so I can spend time with my family." I listen to her words. "So even though what happened to you was the shittiest thing that can happen, there was a reason for it."

"Yeah," I tell her, swallowing the lump, "and I have an even bigger reason to find my father and kill him."

Twelve

CHELSEA

His face goes hard, and I can see the shift happen before my very eyes. "And I have an even bigger reason to find my father and kill him." His voice is cutthroat, and I believe every single word.

I want to say something, but the timer dings, and I turn around, opening the oven door. The heat hits me right away as I grab the oven mitt and pull out the biscuits. The golden brown color is perfect. "I'm going to whip you up some broth." I look over at him, and I see him trying to get up off the couch. I walk over to the fridge, taking the broth I made yesterday for him. I scoop some in a bowl and pop it in the microwave.

"I hate that you have to cook a different meal for me," he says to me. "I'm good with the biscuits and gravy." I stand here looking at him. The ink on his arm is so bright in the light as the sunlight comes into the windows, and he walks into the yellow light.

"How about you wait three days, and then I can make it for you then?" He just nods his head.

"I wish I could help you set up the table or something."

His brown eyes turn a soft green as he stands with the sun on his face. His beard is thicker than it's ever been before. "Where are we going to eat?"

"Let's eat on the couch. I know I said you have to get on your feet, but let's not overdo it. Go sit back down, and I'll bring you your things," I say, walking over to the white cabinet and pulling out two white plates. "We can set you up so it's more comfortable for you." I look over at him and see his leg is shaking just a touch as he puts his hand on the island, trying to put pressure off. "Can you stop being such a macho man and go back to the couch?"

"I'm not being a macho man," he hisses, and I see his chest is heaving like he is panting.

"I know that you think you can just dust yourself off, but you were shot and stabbed." I start to tell him as I plate and then pull open one of the biscuits, and the steam comes out of them. "But your body needs time to heal. Pushing yourself too hard will just set you back down the line."

"I'm not used to just sitting down and doing nothing," he says, and I smile at him.

"Do you want apple juice or orange juice?" I ask, and he sits on a stool at the island.

"Ethan said your biscuits are better than your grandmother's." He smirks at me.

"I learned it from her," I say, breaking open two biscuits and then scooping up the white sausage gravy. "But I've put my own twist on it." I turn back and see that he is looking at me. "Do you need help getting back to the couch?"

"No." He shakes his head, and I just chuckle.

"Okay, macho man," I say, grabbing two forks. "Suit yourself." I watch him turn now and take a step and stop. "Are you sure you don't need help?"

"No," he hisses at me and side-eyes me.

"I would watch that tone, Mayson," I tell him. "I would hate to have you watch me eat this meal."

"You wouldn't do that to me," he says, turning and walking back to the couch. He sits down slowly. I walk to one of the drawers and take out two trays. I put the bowl of broth on his with orange and apple juice. I place my plate on the other one. I carry his first and put it on the table.

"Put your feet up," I tell him, and he turns and puts his feet on the couch, and even though I know he's going to hate it, I put my arm under his feet helping him. "Now, was that so hard?" He glares at me, and I roll my lips. I hand him his tray, grabbing a dish towel and handing it to him. "Did you need a bib?" I hand him his bowl of broth, our fingers grazing when he grabs it from me. I feel the heat from his fingers even when I turn back to grab my own plate.

"That mouth of yours." He shakes his head, looking straight at me. "One of these days, it's going to get you in a world of trouble."

I laugh now, ignoring the way my stomach just flipped as he looked at me. "You see, it shows we've never had a conversation," I tell him, looking sideways at him, cutting a piece of the biscuit. "Because my mouth has been getting me into trouble since I started talking." His eyes on me, I say, "You can only have a bite." I hold the fork up for him, his hand goes to mine on the fork and I try not to shake with nerves from his touch, and he leans in.

"This is good," he says, chewing. "Better than your grandmother's." I smirk at him. "If you tell her that, I'm going to deny it and blame it on the pills you are giving me."

I laugh at him. "I'll just ask them for the tapes." He looks at me. "My house is wired, and everything is recorded." I do a circle with the fork in my hand. His mouth opens and then closes. "Kidding." I point the fork at him.

"Oh, you are bad," he says, shaking his head. "For one second, I believed you."

"I can guarantee you that outside is wired tight," I tell him. "Now the inside." I shrug, taking another bite. "Only time will tell."

He shakes his head and finishes eating his broth. "I have a question."

"I'm full of answers," I tell him, leaning forward and putting my plate on the table.

"When can I shower?" He looks at me.

"Next month." I keep a straight face, seeing the way his mouth just hung open. I smile slyly at him. "To be safe, I would wait until it's fully healed, so maybe even two."

"What?" He gasps. The way his eyes are opened so big, I can't stop the giggle that comes out. "You little shit." He tries to snatch me, but I evade him.

"You can try to catch me," I tell him, bending to take my plate, "but it'll be a cold day before that happens."

He looks at me, his eyes twinkling for the first time. "Is that so?" he says, swinging his feet off the couch. "You sure about that?"

"How about we bet," I tell him, putting the plates in the sink and ignoring the beating of my heart. "When you get better." I fold my arms over my chest. "You do the chase. I bet you won't catch me."

"What do I win?" he asks me. "Usually, when the boy chases the girl, he gets the girl." He limps over a bit. "So what happens if I catch you?"

"Only way to find that out," I say, advancing on him, "is to catch the girl." I see his chest rise and fall. "Now, if you want, I can come in and wash you up."

"Do I look like I need you to give me a sponge bath?" he asks.

"Even tough guys like baths sometimes." I smirk at him.

"Not this tough guy." He folds his arms over his chest now. I take a second to see the orange flower on his arm. The bright green leaves make it pop more.

"Well, then, you can stay dirty," I start to say, and he smiles. "Or..."

"Why?" he moans out. "Why must you put an or in there?"

"Or you can have me sponge you off," I tell him, and he smirks at me.

"You really want to wash me"—he winks at me now—"all you had to do is ask."

"You are lucky you have a bullet wound, and I can't hurt you," I tell him, knowing right now that my cheeks are turning a bright red.

"Thank you," he says softly when I walk back over to him and grab his empty tray.

"You're welcome," I say softly and walk back to the kitchen. He moves his leg now and starts to get up.

"Are you tired?" I ask, and he tries to deny it. "Go rest. I'll come in and check you after.

I'll come and change your bandages." I shake my head.

"Yeah, yeah," he mumbles now as he makes his way back to the bedroom.

"And just for that, I won't even come running if you fall!" I yell to his back.

He laughs, and I don't think I've ever heard him laugh so much since we met. Trust me, I would know since I used to watch him every single fucking time. "You lie."

When he turns and walks back to the bedroom, I ignore that my heart is pounding so hard and so fast it sounds like a group of galloping horses. "What the fuck was that?" I ask, putting my hands to my forehead to check if I have a fever. "Was he flirting with me?" I look back toward the room where he disappeared.

I walk over to the sink and try not to have my head overthink it. He is just being polite, my head says. The conversation plays over and over again in my head, and I'm brought back to the first time my feelings for him went from crush to something else.

I walked into the barn, rubbing my sweaty palms on my jeans. "Oh, I'm sorry," I said, "I didn't know you were in here." I lied straight to his face. I knew exactly where he was. Every single time he came to one of our barbecues, I knew exactly where he was at every single time. I would try and talk to him but all he would give me was a grunt or one-word answers and I was tired of him not seeing me. So I was taking things into my own hands.

"I'm sorry." He stood up from the stool he was sitting on. "I didn't think anyone was going to come in here," he said and just looked at me.

"I was just coming to check on my horse"—I walked over to stand in front of him—"but if you need privacy."

"If anyone should leave, it's me," he said, as he walked over to stand right in front of me. "I just."

"They can be overwhelming"—I smiled at him and he just smirked as he looked down—"but they mean no harm."

"It wasn't your family." His voice came out in a whisper as he looked at me without his stupid glasses. I saw his eyes filled with turmoil and I tilted my head and I wanted to ask him what it was, but Quinn came in and interrupted us.

I blink when the water that is running on my hands turns cold as ice. Turning off the faucet, I gather the dish towel and walk toward the spare bedroom, seeing him in bed with his eyes closed.

I walk back to my bathroom and get two bowls and some towels for when he wakes up. I clean the kitchen, and an hour later, I walk to the bedroom and check on him. I try to be as quiet as I can when I walk in, and his eyes spring open. "I'm so sorry," I tell him, and he rubs his face with his hand. Grabbing the bowl, I make my way to the bathroom and fill it up with warm water.

"I thought you were joking," he says, looking at me coming back with one of the bowls.

"I never joke about sponge baths," I tell him, walking back to grab another bowl. I grab two towels and walk to him. "Turn on your side," I tell him, and he turns on one side, and I tuck a towel under him, repeating it on the other side. "Are you ready?"

"As ready as I'll ever be," he says, and I press the button for his bed to sit up more.

"Can you take off your T-shirt?" I ask him, and he takes it off slowly. I swallow now as I look at him with his shirt off. I put one of the face towels into the hot water and rub the bar of soap on it. "Let me know if this is too hot," I tell him as I put it on his chest. "Good?"

"Yeah," he says, and I tell myself he's just another patient. I tell myself even when my hand shakes as I wash his chest.

"What are you going to do?" I ask him, trying not to embarrass myself while I am washing him. "After all this."

"I have no idea," he says, and his voice sounds tight.

"If you can do anything, what would it be?" I ask him.

"I guess I would do construction," he says. "When I wasn't on tour, I would love building things for the cabin." I look at him.

"What is one thing that you've built?" I ask him as I take a towel in the clean water and rinse him off.

"I built a coffee table," he tells me, and I can see his eyes light up, "then I added two bedrooms to the cabin."

"You like it," I tell him.

"I guess I do," he says. "What about you?"

"I want to get my career going," I tell him, "then I want to do the regular girl things." I smile at him when his eyebrows pull together. "You know, husband and kids." I don't tell him that he's always been the one I've seen holding my hand. I don't tell him that he's the one I've always wanted. Ever since I saw him that first time. "Do you see yourself having children?" I ask him, and I hold my breath now, the thought of him with someone making me feel sick.

"No." He shakes his head. "I've never been in a relationship. I have nothing to bring to the table," he says while I wash up his arm. "I have nothing. The only thing I did have is now burned to the ground." Stopping at his shouler, my face is very close to his.

"Everything can be rebuilt," I tell him in almost a whisper, and he doesn't say anything else. He looks at me and I don't move as my face hovers next to him. I know that if I move even an inch, my lips could be on his. My heartbeat is echoing in my ears. "Do you think you can?" I move away from him now, pointing at his bottom half.

"I got that," he says, and I just nod my head. "Call me when you are done." I walk to the door. "I'm going to leave the door open, but I'll be in the kitchen."

My hands shake as I walk to the kitchen and grab a glass of water. I look out, his words playing over and over in my head. I have nothing. "Stupid man," I mumble.

I walk over to the freezer, taking out a frozen chicken and putting it in a pot of water. This is what I do when I'm stressed, I cook.

"I'm done!" I hear him yelling and walk toward the bedroom. I find him sitting on the bed, his shirt in his hand.

"How was it?" I ask him. When he looks up at me, I can see little drops of water still in his hair.

"Heaven," he says, and I swallow when I see that he's just wearing a pair of black boxers.

"Um, I'll give you a couple of seconds to get dressed," I tell him, turning to walk out of the room.

I look over at him. "Does this offend you?"

I scoff now. "No, of course not." Ignoring the heat rising up my neck.

"I was going to say you already ripped my clothes off me," he jokes, and I just glare at him.

"That was a medical emergency"—I shake my head—"and it's too soon to joke about it." My voice goes soft as I walk over to the supplies. "But I cut them off you. Now lie back."

When I turn back around, he is lying down. I stand next to the bed and bend over. My hand is shaking just a bit. "Chelsea," he says my name softly, and I look up at him. "You saved me."

I swallow down the lump forming in my throat and ignore the stinging of tears in my eyes. It takes me no time to get everything changed and dry, and when I look up, he has his eyes closed. "All done. Did you want a pain pill?" I turn my face to look at him and realize I'm suddenly very close to him. His eyes open, and we stare at each other, and I swear I stop breathing. His hand comes up as he cups one of my cheeks. I don't move. My stomach flips back and forth as his thumb rubs my cheek.

"No pill," he says and then he drops his hand, and the moment is gone.

"I know that you overdid it today." I walk over to throw out the other bandages, then walk back to him and hand him the pain pill with a glass of water.

He takes it without saying anything to me. "Thank you," he says, and I just nod at him and put down the glass.

"I'm going to take a shower," I tell him, and he just looks over at me.

"Leave the door open just in case." He smiles shyly at me, and I walk out of the room with a huge smile on my face as I shake my head.

When I finally get out of the shower and walk into the kitchen, darkness has come. I walk toward his bedroom and see that everything is off. Walking into his room, I see that he is sleeping. A T-shirt covers his chest. I try not to make noise to wake him, and when I get close to the bed, his eyes open if only for a second and then quickly close. "You are what dreams are made of," he says softly and falls back asleep.

Thirteen

MAYSON

"I'*ll kill everything that you love. Nothing is safe from me.*"

My eyes flicker open, and I see darkness again. My eyes roam the four corners of the room and then look out the window. I close my eyes again, and this time I see Chelsea. I was so close to crossing a line yesterday. So close to kissing her that I could have tasted her lips on mine. It was a slip that will never happen again. It can't happen.

Her hands on me as she bathed me made my cock so hard, I was petrified she would see it. Instead, I kept my T-shirt over it in a ball. Listening to her talk about what she wanted in the future and knowing that it was nothing that I could give her. I have nothing to offer her.

I get up slowly as I make my way to the bathroom. The stinging is a bit less today, but it pulls nonetheless. I walk into the kitchen and see that it's just after five in the morning. I see her bedroom door open, and everything inside me tells me not to go there. But before I can think, my feet are walking there, and I see her lying in the middle of the bed. The soft light is on her as she sleeps in a fetal position. Slowly, I close the door, not to wake her, and walk back into the kitchen to start coffee.

Putting my hands down on the counter, I look around her house. Something that I didn't have time to do before. Everything is clean and put in place, the white countertops shine. Two brass lanterns hang from the ceiling that is over the island. She has a small plant sitting on the window ledge that looks out to the backyard, just like her grandmother. A picture of her and her grandmother also on the ledge. I pick it up and hold it in my hand, looking at the smile on Chelsea's face. She is the most beautiful woman I have ever met. I place it back right where I took it from and walk over to the fridge, seeing two color drawings stuck on there.

Grabbing the milk out of the fridge, I walk over to the coffee machine and pour some in. Putting it back into the fridge, I hear soft footsteps. "Hey," she says, wrapping the robe around herself and looking at me with one eye open. "Is everything okay?"

"Yeah," I say, looking at her bare legs now, the robe no longer than the shorts she's wearing underneath it. "I didn't mean to wake you." I grab the coffee in my handm ignoring the little shakes. "Go back to bed. I'll be fine."

"Are you hungry?" She ignores what I just said, walking into the kitchen now. "I can make some eggs. All you ate yesterday was broth." She walks over to the fridge, and I see that her face still has sleep on it. "You can have some solids today."

"Chelsea." I call her name, and she looks over at me. "Go back to bed."

"Do you know," she says, grabbing a pack of bacon out of the fridge, "that breakfast is the most important meal of the day?"

I put my head back and groan. "Do you ever listen?"

She shrugs her shoulders. "At times." She chuckles. "I'm just going to put the bacon in the oven, and then I'm going to have a coffee."

"Whatever I say, you aren't going to listen to me?" I ask her, but I know the answer. It's clear as day she is her own woman, and she does what she wants when she wants it.

"I listen sometimes," she says, starting her own coffee, and I chuckle as I walk to the island and pull out one of the wooden stools.

"Do you have a routine?" I ask her, and she looks over at me.

"Everyone does," she counters as she pours some cream into her coffee. "Even you."

"What's your routine?" I ask her.

"Well, when I get up early before the sun comes up, I make myself a coffee and then go sit on the back steps." She looks toward the back door. "It's pretty amazing to see the sky go from dark to a soft gray, then slowly to a soft purple. Then hitting the trees, making it a light green, right before it turns the whole sky yellow."

"You see the beauty in everything," I say before I can take it back.

"I'm going to grab my coffee and sit outside," she tells me, "and I'm going to do this before you say something that pisses me off." She turns, and I watch her walk out the back door. The robe sways side to side as she walks.

"Fuck," I hiss out, walking over to the door and walking outside. The damp, cold air hits me right away. She doesn't turn her head back to look at me, and it hurts just a touch.

I slowly bend to sit next to her and wince when I finally get to sitting. I don't say anything to her as we sit side by side. I look up at the sky, and I see the darkness slowly turn colors. It's exactly how she said it looked. "You were right," I say, lifting the cup of coffee to my lips. "It really is beautiful." She looks over at me, and my head turns to look at her even though I tell myself not to. The soft blue of her eyes hits me in the stomach as if she just punched me. The breeze blows her hair ever so gently. "It's not the only thing that is beautiful," I tell her and just watch how her mouth opens just a touch. We are lost at this moment, and I feel the pull to her stronger than anything I've ever felt.

"Mayson," she says my name so softly, our faces are moving toward each other. I can taste her lips on mine. When the snap of branches fills the quiet air, my head flies around toward where the noise was coming from. My eyes move around the backyard, and my training kicks in.

The dense trees all the way in the back of the yard make it hard to see anyone there. I stop for a moment and then hear it again. "Get inside," I tell her, my voice tight. "Get inside and get Ethan here." My heartbeat kicks up just a notch, and unlike before, it's not just me this time. I have to protect her.

"I'm not leaving you," she says, and I look over at her and see the fear in her face. But she doesn't leave my side.

"Chelsea," I say between clenched teeth.

"You're wasting time," she says, putting her hand under my arm and lifting me. "Let's go."

My eyes always forward as I stand back up, ignoring the pain from the side. I feel hot drip and know that I popped a stitch for sure. I move back, pushing her inside, walking with my back into the house with my eyes focused to the trees.

"I can't see anything," I hiss out, closing the door, turning to see her with one hand on the island and another hand on her chest. Her head is hanging down. "When I tell you to do something." She turns to look at me, and I see the tears running down her face. "You do it."

"Did you expect me to just leave you out there like a sitting duck." She starts with her voice low, and then it rises. "Abandon you to be shot again." Her chest is panting as if she just ran a mile.

"What good would it do if we were both shot?" I roar out. "How were you going to help me if you got shot and died?"

"What good would it do if I just left you out there and then you died?" she counters me. "I'm going to call Ethan."

I watch her walk away, and my heart starts to slowly calm down, but all I can see is the fear in her eyes. "Keep it calm," I say and look down to see the blood leaking down my leg. "Fuck." I walk over to grab a napkin and wipe the blood. The front door swings open, and I hear boots running. I look up to see that Quinn is standing there, rage on his face now. I've never seen him like this before.

"Where is she?" he asks, looking around.

"She went back to call Ethan." I point at the bedroom.

"She was sobbing," he says, running back to the bedroom, and my heart sinks in my chest. Literally to the fucking floor. I take two steps to her room before the front door opens again and this time it's Ethan who looks like he just rolled out of bed.

"What happened?" he asks, looking around.

"We were outside." I start to tell him, and my eyes go from him to the bedroom, wondering if she's okay. "Watching the sunrise, and we heard snapping coming from the back of the yard. I looked up, but I couldn't see anything."

He takes out his phone and calls someone. "Back of Chelsea's house, I want the feed into the woods," he says, and I hear mumbling on the other line and look down when I feel wet again and see that the blood is now seeping through the shirt. "I want all feeds ready to view when I get there in twenty minutes." He puts the phone back in his pocket.

"Where is Chelsea?" he asks me, and I look down. "What happened?"

"She didn't listen to me when I told her to go inside," I tell him the truth. I leave out that I almost crossed the line with her. I don't tell him that if there wasn't someone in the back, I would have probably kissed her and ruined everything.

"Why doesn't that surprise me." He shakes his head. "Go put on another shirt, and I'll make sure she is okay."

I nod at him. "Maybe she'll listen to you," I huff out and walk to the bedroom, but with the pulling of the stitches in my legs and my side, it takes more time than I want it to.

I peel off the shirt and look down, seeing the bandage soaked through. "Mother." I stop talking when I peel the bandage off and see two of the dark stitches come right out, and I know I have to tell her.

I turn and walk out of the room, and I know that I should wait for her in my room. I know that I should give her time. I'm in the hallway when I hear Ethan. "It isn't my story to tell, Chelsea."

"Do you know how scared I was out there with him?" she says, and whatever I thought we had is gone with just those words. "He's here in the house with me, and this morning, I thought he was going to be shot again," she says, her voice low but still loud enough for me to hear. "How do you want me to handle that?" I close my eyes and turn around, walking back to the bedroom.

Grabbing a bandage, I press down on it, and the pain rips through to the other side of me. I have to sit down, and I see Ethan stick his head in. "We are going to head out. I'll be back with Casey in a bit to tell you what we found." I nod at him. "She's getting dressed, and she'll be right in. I told her about the bleeding."

I don't say anything to him because there are no words to say. I can't say anything; all I can do is get far away from here and her.

Fourteen

CHELSEA

"Are you going to be okay here by yourself?" Quinn asks me, standing at the entrance to my bedroom. Ethan just walked out.

"I'll be okay," I tell him. "It was just a bit too much," I tell him, and I close my eyes. "I have to make sure he's not bleeding too much."

"You call me if you need me," he says, and I just nod at him. Maybe it wasn't a good idea to call him after Ethan, but I didn't know what else to do. My heart was beating so fast and my whole body was shaking uncontrollably. I was afraid he would walk into the room and see me, so I called the only person I knew who would be here in no time. I was not wrong. He was here in under a minute. I was lucky he was already in the barn working out. I guess it was my lucky day in a way.

I grab a pair of baggy black pants that are tight around my ankles with a white short-sleeved shirt. I tuck it in the front and tie my hair on top of my head. I don't bother washing my face before going back to him, and I can only imagine how I look.

I find him sitting on the bed, his head down as he puts pressure on the wound. "Hey," I say softly, and he looks up and just the look of him is like you cut off both my legs. Maybe I should have washed my face. I'm sure my nose is red from the crying, and my eyes are puffy.

"Are you in pain?" I ask, and he just shakes his head.

"I'm actually numb," he says. "But I think two stitches came out."

I walk over and put on gloves, going back over to him. "I'm going to need you to lie down."

"I'm so sorry," he says, not moving, his head moving up, and I see the tears in his eyes. I want to tell him that he has nothing to be sorry for. "You asked Ethan about my story."

"I," I start to say. "I know your father tortured you, but I was asking him why."

"I thought you heard me tell the story," he says, and I shake my head.

"I only heard the end of it. When you told them the day Braxton died," I say his real name, and it feels wrong on my lips.

He shakes his head. "You missed the best part of the story," he says sarcastically. "When I was five years old," he starts talking, "my mother was reading a book to me, and my father came in. He was usually never around except for dinnertime. But this time, it was the middle of the afternoon. Or at least I think it was, then I had just come home from school." His eyes look up at me. "I knew something was off because he wobbled a bit when he came in, and I remember my mother telling me to go to my room."

"You don't have to do this," I tell him, not sure I can handle this.

"You deserve to know," he says. "If anyone deserves to know my story, it's you. You saved me. And in return, I've put a bull's-eye on your back." He looks up at the ceiling now. "I whined when she stopped reading to me. My father turned around and slapped me so hard I flew across the room." I can't stop the gasp that comes out of me. "My mother ran to me instead of going to my father. He beat her right next to me. That is my first memory. I tried to take care of her. She would get up and make sure to make him breakfast and dinner. But when he left, she would sleep the whole day. I would lie next to her, and the bruises faded from a deep purple to a green to a yellow. When you described the sunrise before, all I could do was see her bruises in my head."

I put my hand to my stomach, hoping I don't get sick in front of him. "Mayson," I say his name in a whisper.

"I never whined again. Never made another noise, and when he would come in from work, I would hide in a corner, hoping it wouldn't happen again," he says as a tear runs down his face. "But it was not the last time that he beat my mother. I would listen to see if maybe she said something that would set him off, but I understood things more as I got older. I knew that when he was having a bad day, he would make sure she did also. Her beatings would tell you how bad of a day he was having. If he hit her less than five times, he was just irritated. If it went on for over an hour, it was a rough day. If he spent the whole night taking shots at her, you knew that it was a bad fucking day." I can't stop the tears from falling down my face. "He was six foot one and weighed two hundred and forty-five pounds. She was five foot two and weighed under a hundred pounds. She would fly like a rag doll. Imagine being ten years old and telling your mother what position to get into when your father was kicking her. I would try to clean up when she was in bed, but there wasn't anything that I could do to stop the roaches from coming in. No matter how much I tried."

"You were trying to protect her," I tell him, not even trying to hide the tears.

"Protect her." He shakes his head. "When I was fourteen,

he hit her so hard she dislocated her shoulder." I close my eyes, knowing what he's going to say next. "I had to snap it back into place. My mother howled out in so much pain she passed out." His own tears are running down his face. "When she died, I sold her wedding ring so I could buy her flowers." He turns his hand now, showing me the orange on his arm. This is for her." He rubs it, and I walk over to him, my fingers roaming with his. "Birds of paradise."

"It's beautiful," I tell him, and he looks up at me.

"After she was gone, there was no one to take the beatings but me," he says, and I stand here in the middle of his legs. "It started slow, a smack here and there. I would duck, but it would just make it worse." He grabs my hand and brings it to his other arm. The American flag tattoo bright with colors. He moved my hand down a scar now. "He tore open my arm with a broken beer bottle. He only took me to the hospital because he couldn't stop the bleeding. Told them I fell and landed on the broken glass. It was the first tattoo I got." My eyes look at the tattoo and I want to kiss the scar that lives under there.

"I'm so sorry," I tell him.

"I thought families like yours only existed on television or in books," he says. "The first time I came here I was blown away. The love that you all had for each other was contagious. I just stood there and took it all in. Basked in it and pretended that I was one of you. I thought about how different my life would have been had I been raised with this kind of love."

"You are one of us," I say, ignoring all the warning signs that are flashing. I wipe away one of his tears.

"I can't stay here," he says when I cup his cheek. "I refuse to see that fear in your eyes."

"I was scared," I admit. "Scared that you would be hurt again. I was scared that this time I wouldn't be able to save you." My other hand comes out, and my thumb catches a lone tear.

"I won't let you be hurt." He swallows. "I can't. I wouldn't be able to live with myself."

"Then stay," I whisper, and I don't know exactly what I'm asking him. My heart knows, but so does my head. "Stay and let us protect you." He looks up at me. "Stay and let us be by your side."

I feel his hand on my leg now. "Chelsea, I won't be able to survive if anything happens to you."

"I won't be able to survive if you leave," I tell him honestly, and I take the biggest leap of my life. I bend down and whisper, "Don't leave me."

"Chelsea," he says to me right before my lips touch his. My tongue comes out to touch his, and all of my fears, thoughts, and everything I thought I knew are forgotten, and the only thing that matters is him and me. One of his hands comes up now, going to my head, tilting it just a bit. The kiss deepens as our tongues fight with each other.

I finally let go of his lips, the both of us looking at each other without saying a word. "Chelsea." He says my name again, and I'm afraid he will tell me this will never happen again. I'm afraid he's going to tell me the kiss I've been waiting for, for the last seven years was a mistake.

"I should check your wound," I tell him, walking away, my hands shaky now. "Lie on the bed." He does what he's told, and I avoid looking at him. "You popped three stitches," I tell him as the blood drips out.

"I thought so," he says, and I walk over, grabbing a needle.

"I'm going to numb you." I work without making eye contact with him. I wash and stitch him back up. "Now, can you try not to tear them again?"

He just nods his head. "Go shower, and I'm going to go and make breakfast, and we can start the day over." I run out of the room, going to the kitchen, and only when I hear the water start in the bathroom do I let my head hang.

The tension from my whole body slowly leaves me, and my knees buckle when I hear his words over and over in my head, how different one person's life can be from another. I make breakfast in record time, and when he comes out, he moves slower than he did before. "You're done."

"I am," he says, stopping in front of the island. "We should talk."

"No," I tell him, and his eyes go big. "I think we did enough talking for the day." I swallow, and I grab two plates. "I just have one more thing to say."

"You always have to have the last word." He shakes his head.

"I'm going to make you see the beauty in it." I swallow down the lump forming in my throat, worrying that I might upset him but wanting him to know.

"In what?" he asks, confused.

I put the plates down on the counter. "In the colors of the sunrise."

Fifteen

MAYSON

I watch her put the plates down and look at me, and my heart speeds up when she looks down nervously and then back up again. I don't know what I'm waiting to hear. "In the colors of the sunrise." It's a good thing I'm holding on to the counter, or I think my legs would give out. "Every day, we are going to sit outside and watch the beauty of it."

I shake my head, not sure any words can come out over the lump in my throat. My mouth also feels like it's dry as the desert on a summer day. "Let's sit and eat," she says, plating eggs, bacon, sausage, and toast.

I walk around the counter to her, and she turns, looking at me. My hand comes up without even thinking about it, and my thumb rubs her chin softly. "I don't think it's a good idea," I finally say.

"What exactly isn't a good idea?" She steps in closer to me, and all I can focus on is her lips. All I want is to taste her again, if only one more time. I move my nose against hers softly, and she moves her head back just a touch. Her hand comes up, and she touches my face, her thumb rubs my lower lip. "Will you kiss me, Mayson?" she asks me in the softest, sweetest voice I've ever heard. Her words are like an angel.

I know I shouldn't. I know deep down that I should turn and walk back into the room and forget our first kiss altogether. Forget the way she felt in my arms, forget the way she looks at me. Forget the way I want to make everything shine around her. Forget that I want to be that better person, not just for me anymore but for her. I lick my lips and lean in just a touch more as her eyes slowly close. "Che—" I start to say her name, and then we both hear the crushing of rocks in the driveway followed by two car doors slamming. I move away from her, our hands falling to the sides of us.

The door swings open, and I see that it's Ethan followed by Casey, and they both look at us. I look down, afraid he is going to see I took advantage of his sister. "Hey," Casey says, coming over to the kitchen.

Chelsea smiles at him and walks around the island, going to her uncle and hugging him. Ethan just stares at me. "Did you want a cup of coffee?" Chelsea asks Casey.

"No," he says. "Mayson." I look over at him. "We need to talk."

"Okay," I say, looking at him and then looking back at Ethan. "Let's hear it."

"Why don't we..." Ethan starts, looking at me and then looking at Chelsea.

"Oh, you did not just do that," Chelsea says, folding her arms over her chest. "You did not come into my house"—she points at the floor—"and dismiss me like that, Ethan McIntyre."

"Oh, shit. She used your whole name," Casey says. "If she is anything like her momma, that means you're in trouble." He puts his hands on his hips, looking at both of them.

I fold my arms over my chest and wait to see what Ethan

says. "You were the one who didn't want to be involved." He points at her.

"And you were the one who put me in the middle of this." She advances on him. "So now is not the time for you to try to protect me."

"She's right," I hear myself say, and all sets of eyes swing my way. "She's in this all the way."

Ethan shakes his head. "This is a bad idea," he mumbles.

"Did you find anything from the woods?" I ask, not sure I can take much more of not knowing.

"Nothing," Ethan says. "We checked everything, but we can't see that far out."

"We are fixing that today," Casey says now. "I am having cameras installed all over this place. If a fucking squirrel eats a leaf, I'm going to find it."

I look at them, and I can feel I'm missing something. "What are you not telling me?"

"We found a couple of things," Casey says, and I can tell he doesn't know how to start.

"When was the last time you used the name Braxton?" he asks, and my eyebrows pinch together at his question.

"I paid forty-seven dollars and twelve cents to change my name. I never used it again. Even when I joined the military, I used Mayson." I look at them both. "Why?"

"Seems like Braxton Michaels has left a hefty paper trail for the past eight years," Casey says. "How many credit cards do you have?"

"Zero." I fold my arms over my chest. "Pay cash for everything."

"According to your credit report, you have over thirty different credit cards," Ethan says. "All maxed out. All in collections."

"How the fuck can that happen?" I ask, and they exchange a look. My pulse kicks up a bit as I process the information.

"We need some answers," Ethan says.

"You aren't the only one who needs fucking answers!" I almost shout. "I've kept my head down, and I never applied for a credit card. I don't even have a fucking bank loan for the cabin." My hands go to my hips, and I try to reel in my anger.

"How is that possible?" Chelsea asks.

"I gave Ethan a good chunk down, and I paid him monthly." I swallow down. "With interest."

Ethan nods. "I have one bank account that my money is deposited to and that's it."

I close my eyes now, the pounding in my head getting even worse. "In case you guys missed the memo, I don't do material things. I have enough clothes for a week. That's it. I have a truck that is paid for and the cabin." I look at Chelsea now. "Other than that, I have nothing." My pride be damned at this point. I have nothing to offer her. I have nothing to give her. I am nothing.

"There is more," Ethan says, his voice going low.

"How can there possibly be fucking more?" My voice is tight. My heart is pounding so fast it is going to look like I'm panting in a minute. "What else can there be?"

"We just scratched the surface," Casey says. "You have over twenty-seven apartments that you rented in twelve years."

"I've been on tour seven times," I tell them. "I signed up for every tour I was offered. When I was home, it was for a couple of weeks at a time, and I stayed in motels. Again, paid in cash."

"Does the name Rosalie Henderson ring a bell?" Casey asks, and I shake my head.

"Not in the least," I tell them, and I look over at Chelsea, who just looks down now. Her hands are now wringing together.

"Braxton Michaels married her four years ago." I stare at him, my mouth going open.

"Excuse me," Chelsea says, walking toward her bedroom. I want to chase after her, but I know that if I do, there will be even more questions, and I definitely don't have the answers to those either.

"Wait!" I shout, and she stops mid-step. "I don't know her," I say.

Ethan looks at me and then looks at his sister, and from one look, he knows something is up. "I mean, she was thirty-five," he says, and Chelsea turns around.

"Well, did anyone go to her and find out who she is?" I ask. "Do we have an address? Let's go find her, and she can tell you she didn't marry me." I look at them back and forth.

"She died two years ago," Ethan says, and he looks down and then up again. "Left at the emergency room hospital. Beaten so bad her head was mush."

"Oh my god," Chelsea says and puts her hands to her mouth.

"My father," I finally say, everything fucking clicks into place. "My father stole my identity." Rage rips through me. "I never even thought about it."

"That is what we think, too," Casey says. "I have my guys going through all the paper trail. But I'm going to be honest, there is a fuck ton of it."

"Great," I say, shaking my head and wiping my face with my hands. "Just fucking great. This makes no fucking sense." I look at everything. "I was so fucking careful. I covered my tracks. How did he find me?"

"That is what we are trying to find out. I will let you know when I have something else," Casey says, and he turns to walk out of the house. Stopping at Chelsea, he whispers something in her ear. She smiles at him, nodding her head.

"I have a bag in the car," Ethan says. "More clothes since you can't stop fucking up the ones I already gave you." He turns to walk out of the house, leaving Chelsea and me alone.

"Now do you see?" I look at her as soon as the front door closes, and I know I don't have much time. It isn't going to take him long to get the bag and come back. I am not wrong, I don't even have time to say anything else.

He walks back in with a green Army bag so full the zipper doesn't close. "My mother," Ethan starts to say. "Well, she found out, and things just got out of hand. She called the girls, and they went on a buying spree. They did it in turns so no one would be on to them." Chelsea laughs, closing her eyes and holding her forehead. "I'm not even kidding. They thought they were so smooth. But they went to the same store." I want to laugh at that one.

"Let me know how much I owe you," I tell him as he just laughs.

"Have you not met my mother?" he asks me, and he just shakes his head. "She won't take a penny from you."

"But..." I start to say.

"But nothing," Chelsea says now. "It's rude to say no to a gift. It's their Southern charm."

"I'm going to head out and pass by the command post," he says, and I nod at him.

He walks out, and I stand here in the middle of Chelsea's house. "We need to talk," I tell her.

"Yeah," she says, and I can tell she is ready for a fight. Her shoulders go square, and her back goes tight. "We do."

"Good." I swallow the lump that has risen from my stomach to my throat. "So you understand."

"Oh, I understand all right," she says, not moving from her spot. I just look at her blue eyes and her lips that I want to spend the night kissing. "The question is, do you understand?" I look at her, not really knowing what is going on. "Before you asked me 'now do you see.'" She doesn't even give me a chance to say anything. "I see everything very clear, do you?"

"Yeah, I do, and it's fucking bleak," I answer her.

"Then we aren't looking at the same thing," she says, and she comes to me now. I should move away from her, but my feet feel like they are stuck in concrete blocks. "This is what I see," she tells me, standing chest to chest with me. I look down at her as she looks up. "I see someone who was dealt a bad fucking hand." My eyes stare right into hers. "I see a man who has risen from the hell he has been in. I see a man who deserves all the colors in the world." She steps even closer to me. "I see a man who deserves all the love in the world." Her hand comes up to cup my face. "I see a man who deserves people who stand with him and protect him." I want to say something to her, but nothing comes out. "I see a man who deserves everything."

Sixteen

CHELSEA

I look into his eyes and lay it all out for him, his eyes filling with water. "You and me, we see different things."

I put my hands on his chest, and I can feel his heartbeat racing just as fast as mine is. "Well, then we see two different things," I say softly. "Just like the sunrise." The same sunrise we've been watching for the past week and a half.

"I can't give you what you want," he says, looking at me, his eyes almost dark from his emotions. "I have nothing for you," he says, the last words going lower. "And you"—he pushes back the hair from my face—"you deserve to have someone who can give you everything."

His hand goes to my cheek, and I feel his fingers on my face. My whole body wakes up. My hand leaves his face and goes to the wrist that is holding my face. "I'm looking at him," I whisper. His head turns to the side now, and our lips hover so close to each other.

He's going to have to make the move, I tell myself. It's up to him if this kiss is going to happen. I need to know he wants to kiss me as much as I want to kiss him. Our mouths open as he slowly closes the distance, and his tongue comes out. My tongue slides with his as his hands move from my face to my hair. He cups my head in his hands as he deepens the kiss. He closes his mouth a bit, turning to the other side, and my hand comes up to hold his face. His beard makes my hand tingle as the butterflies in my stomach flutter everywhere.

"Chelsea." He says my name now in almost a plea when he lets go of my lips for just a second but then comes back to kiss me. His tongue comes out to play with mine once again, and my arms wrap around his neck. My eyes fly open when he stops kissing me but doesn't move away from me. "This is wrong." He looks at my lips. "I'm too old for you."

"This," I tell him, swallowing, and rubbing my nose with his, then kissing his lips softly, "is the smartest thing I've ever done." I kiss him again. "I've waited a long time to take that chance and kiss you," I say, going back to his lips. "Every single time I saw you, I would think about how it would be like to hold your hand. To lean over and kiss you." He looks at me, and I hope he hears my words.

The front door opens, and I jump away from him. "Hello," I hear Amelia say as she walks into the room, both of us standing close to each other. Her eyes go from me to Mayson. "Hey," she says. "The door was open." She uses her thumb to point over her shoulder. "I'm sorry. I can come back."

"No," I say, my voice coming back to me. "It's fine. I was just checking his bandages."

"I was wondering if you wanted to go for some lunch." Amelia comes in more now. She is the same age as I am, so we grew up more like sisters than cousins.

"You should go," Mayson says, and I look over at him.

"I'm not leaving you here alone," I tell him, then I turn back to look at Amelia, who is watching our exchange with eagle eyes. "I can't leave him alone."

"No problem," she says. "Quinn is on his way."

"There, I won't be alone," he says. "I'll be fine."

"Go change," Amelia says, and I look over at her and glare. "You have blood on your shirt." I look down and see that I have a couple of spots of blood.

"Fine, I'll go change." I look at her. "There is still breakfast on the counter," I tell Mayson, who nods at me and walks over to the island. Amelia looks at him and then at me. Her eyebrows rise, and I just shake my head. I turn around and walk to my bedroom, knowing I will have to talk eventually.

I slip on my khaki linen shorts and grab a white sleeveless shirt, tucking it in the front. I slip on my caramel Tory Burch flip-flops. Walking to the bathroom, I wash my face and look at the little red spots around my lips from his beard. I smile if just for a minute and then tie my hair back.

When I make my way back to the kitchen, I see Amelia is standing in the back of the island chatting with Mayson, and she throws her head back and laughs. She smiles when she sees me. "Ready?"

"Yeah," I say. "Can we wait for Quinn?" I ask, walking to sit on the stool next to Mayson.

"I'm here," Quinn says, coming in the front door. He looks at us. "You can go now."

"Jesus Christ," Mayson mumbles, and I look over at him. He looks sideways at me. "I don't need a babysitter."

"I'm not babysitting anyone," Quinn says, going to the fridge, opening it, and sticking his head inside. Grabbing the plate of pie I have in there, he asks, "Is there ice cream?"

"As if I would have apple pie without ice cream," I say, getting up now. "If you need me, call me," I say, grabbing my purse. I take one more look at Mayson before turning to walk out of the house.

"So," Amelia says from beside me, and I look over at her. Her blond hair is blowing in the wind.

"Can we get into the car first before you start?" I ask, not looking at her as she laughs. "I hate you." I open her truck door and get in.

"You hate me because I see right through all the bullshit." She chuckles, starting the truck and not saying a word.

I look out at the trees as we drive into town. My eyes roam everywhere now as I try to see if anything is in the dense trees. You can't see shit, and I close my eyes as the sun hits my face.

We get to the diner, and I get out of her truck. This diner has been around since our parents were in high school. It's the place to be Friday night right before the football game or Saturday night if the fair comes to town. "I'm going to get a cheeseburger," I say as I slam the door shut. "With sweet potato fries," I tell her, laughing, and feel eyes on me. I turn around but seeing no one there, I tell myself it's all in my head.

Walking into the diner, I say hello to mostly everyone. Living in a small town, you know everyone. There are no secrets in small towns, and if there are, eventually they come to light.

"Good morning, beautiful girls," Heloise says, coming over to us. "I'll get you two strawberry milkshakes in just a minute," she says, walking past us now toward another table.

"Do you think she'll ever see us as grown-ups?" Amelia asks me, looking around. "So what's new?"

"Oh, fuck off," I say under my breath, looking around to see if anyone is out of the normal. If there is a weird face anywhere.

"Such language for the perfect child." She makes fun of me, and I glare. "But honestly, are you okay?"

"No," I say, avoiding her eyes and grabbing the menu that hasn't changed in over twenty years. "And I know what you're going to say."

"Really?" She sings the word. "And what do you think I'm going to say?"

"That it's stupid to get involved," I say, my eyes roaming

over the menu. "That I shouldn't go there, and that I'm only going to get my heart broken."

"Among other things," she says, and I know she's staring at me. "It's dangerous." I shake my head. "Okay, I know you've been hot for him since, I don't know, you were eighteen, but we always knew he was hiding something."

"Um, we did not." I scoff at her. "We thought he was mysterious."

"You thought he was mysterious." She points at me. "I thought he was creepy." I glare at her. "I mean, he was always hot but creepy."

I laugh now and don't say anything to her because Heloise puts the milkshakes in front of us.

"I have your cheeseburgers coming up," she says, walking away.

"I guess we both get cheeseburgers," I say, looking down. "I like him a lot. I always have." I look at her, and she tilts her head to the side. "Oh, I always thought he was hot."

"Do you think he knows?" she asks me, and I shake my head.

"How could he know anything?" I tell her. "He's busy trying to be the man he already is." I shake my head. "He brought Grandma flowers last year when he came to visit. She blushed, and he didn't even see it. He's oblivious," I admit. "He's oblivious to any good deed he's ever done because he's too busy thinking of that one bad one. He carried Gabriel in his arms for two hours because he fell asleep and he didn't want to wake him up. Or when he stayed two days to help Grandpa build a fence." I look at her. "He's the man he wants to be," I say softly.

"You think you can make him see?" she asks, and I look out of the window now. I suddenly feel eyes on me, and I look back into the restaurant. My eyes roam around, seeing if anyone is looking at me.

The front door opens, and my heart is beating so fast I almost jump out of my seat when I see the new barn manager come in. Asher spots us and holds up his cowboy hat. "Holy shit," I hear Amelia mumble and look over at her. "Is he coming over here?"

My eyes go big when I look back and see him coming to the table now. "Afternoon, ladies," he says, his accent very, very soft.

"Hey, Asher," I say. "How are you settling in?" He started working for my uncle Casey a month ago.

"Starting to feel like home," he says and looks over at Amelia, giving her a small smile. "If you'll excuse me, I have to get food for the boys." He turns on his cowboy boots and walks to the counter.

"He's a strange one," I say as I watch him.

"He is not," Amelia says, and it's my turn to look at her now.

"Interesting," I say to her and laugh. It's her turn to glare. "You know that your father—"

"Okay," she says, putting her hands on the table.

"I'm going to go and order Mayson something," I tell her, and she just nods at me. I get up, and I can swear I still feel eyes on me. I look around as I walk to the counter. Asher grabs the big box of takeout containers and then smiles at me when he walks away. He takes one final look at Amelia before walking out. I order a cheeseburger to go and walk back to the table.

"What's wrong?" Amelia asks me as I sit down.

"I feel like I'm being watched," I tell her, looking around. "It's probably all in my head."

Heloise brings me the container, and I smile at her, and we walk out of the diner. The wind blows my hair back as I look over to the side and see a man standing just looking at me. I stop walking when a school bus driver stops right in front of him.

"What's the matter?" she asks, and when the school bus leaves, the man is gone.

"There was a man there." I point at where the man was standing. "Did you not see him?" I look around, going into a circle as my hands start to shake. "He was right there." I point at the empty space where there are only trees now. "Did you see him?"

"No," Amelia says, coming to grab my hand. "Let's go now." She pulls me toward the truck now. My feet move as fast as I can while looking around to see if the man is there again.

We walk back toward her truck, and I get in. My eyes go everywhere once I get inside the truck. I look everywhere as she pulls out of the diner parking lot. When she turns, I can see someone in the woods. "There!" I shout at her, and she looks over, and he's gone again. "He was right there."

Seventeen

MAYSON

I sit at the counter and finish my food right next to Quinn. Neither of us says a word, and the food feels like a brick in my stomach.

I toss the food around on my plate, waiting for Quinn to say something, knowing he has things to say. I get up, walking over to the sink and turn the water on to rinse off my plate.

"If you hurt her..." Quinn says, and I look over my shoulder at him. I turn off the water and put the dish in the dishwasher.

"I have no idea what you mean." I avoid his eyes. Quinn and I have always been cordial at best. We even shared a laugh a couple of times. But we've never been best friends.

"You can't be that stupid," he says, putting down the spoon in his hand.

I turn, leaning on the counter, and cross my legs at the ankle. "Again," I say, "I have no idea what you mean."

"You had to have seen it." He looks straight at me. "She would always use excuses to be next to you." I swallow now, and I don't say anything, giving him ample time to say more. "Like coming to the barn to check on her horse when you were in there." I remember exactly what he's talking about, but I don't tell him anything. "Every time you came to one of the Sunday dinners, she would always be right there next to you."

"Doesn't mean nothing," I tell him.

He pushes off from the island and comes over, putting his plate in the dishwasher. "If she gets hurt," he says, his tone tight, "no one is going to save you from me."

"If she gets hurt," I say the words, the burning coming to my stomach, "someone is going to die."

I push off from the counter now and walk over to the bedroom. Sitting on the bed, I put my head back, looking at the ceiling, and close my eyes. I knew the game she was playing. I knew the signs. I just didn't know that someone else was watching. I would always look around when it was the two of us, looking to make sure that no one was watching us. Usually, it would be just Amelia.

I'm about to lie back on the bed when I hear the crushed rocks and the sound of running. My heart speeds up, and I jump up, almost running out of the room when the front door swings open.

Her face is filled with tears, but it's her eyes that make me take a step back. Filled with fear. Filled with confusion. Filled with all the things that they shouldn't be filled with.

Quinn is beside me and now past me to stop her. "I saw," she says, now hyperventilating. I look over at Amelia, who is looking out the front door right and left and then closing the door.

"What the fuck happened?" I shout.

"I saw..." Chelsea starts to say, but no words are coming out. She puts her hands on her knees as she tries to get the words out.

"She saw someone," Amelia says, and the hair on the back of my neck stands up. I look over at her, and she puts her hands up. "I didn't see him."

"Yeah, it's me," Quinn says, and I turn to look at him holding a phone to his ear. "There is a situation at Chelsea's." He looks over at me, the look telling me shit is about to go down. "Call your dad."

He puts the phone back in his jeans, and I finally snap out of it and walk over to Chelsea. I squat down in front of her, ignoring the pull of my bandages on my legs. "Hey," I say, and she just looks at me, shaking her head. "Just breathe," I tell her. "Breathe with me. In." I inhale with her. "Exhale." She copies me now. "That's it, you can do it with me."

"What do you mean she freaked out?" I hear Quinn ask Amelia, and then I look over at them. They both stop talking.

I turn back to look at Chelsea. "Just breathe, baby. I have you," I say softly so just she can hear me. Her breathing starts to come back to normal when the door swings open, and her eyes go big as she turns to look at the door. I get up as Jacob, Ethan, and Beau run into the house.

"Where is my dad?" Quinn asks.

"He's going to be here in five minutes," Beau says, rushing over and taking Chelsea in his arms. "I'm here," he tells her, and I want to brush her hair away from her face so I can see her eyes. I want her to know I'm here and nothing is going to happen to her.

"What's going on?" Ethan says, looking around and then sees a trickle of blood run down my leg. I shake my head slowly, telling him not now.

"We might as well wait for Uncle Casey," Amelia says, and she is in Jacob's arms as he kisses her head.

"I need water," Chelsea says, and she pushes away from her father and slowly walks to the kitchen. I follow her, and Ethan just watches us. She grabs a bottle of water, and her hands shake as she tries to bring it to her mouth.

The front door opens, and Casey comes in, putting his sunglasses on the top of his head.

"Okay, we are all here," I say now. "What happened?"

Everyone looks at Chelsea. "We went to the diner," she says. "We were sitting at the booth, and I just felt eyes on me the whole time," she says, and the blood flowing in my body turns to ice. "I kept looking around the whole time to see if someone was in the diner I didn't know." Jacob looks over at Casey, who nods his head. "Asher came in, and I got up to order some food to bring back here," she says. Her hands shake just a bit, and she shakes them off.

"You can do this," I say to her softly. "Just focus."

"We walked out of the diner, and I just felt it." She looks at me now. "I saw a man. I don't even know what he looked like anymore." She closes her eyes. "But he was just staring at me."

"Did you go up to him?" Ethan asks. "Did you talk to him?"

"No." Chelsea shakes her head. "A bus came by, and by the time it left, he wasn't there anymore." She puts her hands on her stomach. "I thought at that point that I had made it up." Her lower lip shakes. "I thought it was all in my head. I ran to the truck, got in, and I kept looking around, but nothing was there. It was just all in my head, I thought. But..." She looks at me. "But then when we were pulling out, I saw him again. His beady eyes were staring straight at me."

"That motherfucker!" I roar out and look over at the men. "We need to find him and end this. Do you hear me?" I walk back to the bedroom and pick up the green bag Ethan tossed me earlier. I ignore the pain in my body. I ignore my whole body going into shutdown. I ignore the pain in my heart piercing so hard you would think I was shot straight in the chest.

"What are you doing?" Chelsea asks, her voice frantic.

"I'm doing what I should have done two days ago," I tell the whole room. "I'm getting out of here."

"And where are you going to go?" Chelsea's voice comes out angrily.

"Anywhere but here," I tell her and look at Casey. "You can get me set up somewhere off the grid."

"I can," Casey says to me, looking down before continuing. "But."

"No more fucking buts!" I roar out. "He could have hurt her and then what?" All the men look down at the floor. Just the thought of her being hurt because of me is too much to bear. I can't do it. I won't do it.

"Before you decide anything," Jacob says, "this could work to our advantage." I put my hands on my head in shock.

"You have got to be fucking kidding me," Beau finally says. "He got close enough to her that she felt fucking eyes on her." He points at Chelsea. "How much fucking closer does he have to get before we listen to Mayson and get him out of here?"

"We don't even know if it's him," Ethan says calmly. "No one knows for sure."

"Who the fuck else could it be?" Quinn asks, his voice going louder.

"Let us check the tapes and decide then," Casey says. "If it is him, we can come up with a plan to bring him out."

"You want us to play sitting possum?" I shake my head now. "So just sit here waiting for him to strike."

"It's not the dumbest plan," Ethan says. "We have something he doesn't."

"Yeah, and what is that?" I ask him, furious now.

"We got eyes on him," Ethan says. "He doesn't have a game plan."

"He came out in the daytime," I say to him. "He came out into the light and she saw him." I point at Chelsea. "He had to have known she would see him and tell me."

"Exactly," Ethan says. "He knew she would come back and tell you. He knew you would leave here."

"He's right," Jacob says now. "You will be playing into his hands."

"So what does this mean?" I look around at everyone.

"It means you have no choice but to stay," Quinn says, shaking his head and looking down at his feet with his hands on his head.

"You guys have twenty-four hours," I say with my teeth clenched. "Twenty-four hours to find him. After that, I'm playing this game on my own."

Eighteen

CHELSEA

"You guys have twenty-four hours." I look over at Mayson, his hands and teeth clenched. "Twenty-four hours to find him. After that, I'm playing this game on my own." If I didn't fear him before and I didn't know him, I would be scared. I would be very scared.

"I'm going to go back to the station," my uncle Jacob says. "I'm going to get extra eyes on the house tonight."

"I'm going to go and pack her bag," my father says, and I just look at him. Everyone looks over at him. "He needs to stay here." He points at Mayson. "That doesn't mean she needs to stay here with him."

"He's right," Mayson says just as I say, "Absolutely not."

All eyes turn to me. "I am not leaving my home," I say softly, and my father starts to shake his head. "I am not leaving my fucking house."

"Chelsea," Mayson says, almost as a warning.

I shake my head hard now. "I am not going to leave my home," I tell him. "I am not leaving here because this is my home. So if this man who was watching me thinks he's going to just come into my house." I laugh, and if I didn't know

112

myself, I would say I sound like I'm losing it. And maybe I am losing it. "I don't know who the man was. I don't know what he wanted. But I know one thing. I'm not letting him scare me out of my house." I look over at Mayson, hoping he can read between those lines. Because what I really want to say is I'm not leaving you.

"Five minutes ago, you couldn't even breathe," Quinn says, and I glare at him.

"Well, now I'm fine," I say through clenched teeth. "I'm going to change," I tell the room, "and I think everyone has something to do." I look at Amelia. "Bring the food in."

I turn and walk toward my bedroom, and I'm not surprised that Amelia and Quinn both follow me into my bedroom. "You guys," I say, turning on them and see that Quinn has closed the door.

"This stops now," Quinn says to me. "You can not stay here."

"I, for once, agree with Quinn," Amelia says. "You can let him stay here. But you." She points at me. "You need to pack a bag and come stay with me. The guys can get someone else to come in here."

"I can stay here," Quinn says, and I look at him.

"You are one second away from shooting him yourself." I point at him.

"I won't hurt him." He smirks now. "If anything, you can always fix him up."

"That isn't funny." I close my eyes and sit on the bed.

Amelia comes over and puts her arm around me. "I know you want to help."

"It's more than that," I tell her and look over at Quinn. "I know you think I'm just some stupid kid with a crush, and I'll get over it. But..."

"Nothing we can say will make you change your mind?" Quinn asks, and I know I don't even have to answer him.

"Jesus, you two have been a pain in my ass since I was five years old." Amelia and I both laugh. "Why can't you just be like normal girls who chase cowboys and listen to the men?"

I raise an eyebrow. "Quinn Barnes," I say. "I'm gonna tell your momma what you just said."

"Yeah." He smirks at me. "When you do, make sure you do it with my father there."

"Get out." I point at the door.

"I'll be outside," he says.

"Peeping Tom!" I tell him, and he turns to walk out of the room.

"I'm going to be okay," I tell Amelia and look at her.

"You didn't see how freaked out you were today." She blinks away tears. "I just don't want..."

"He won't let anything happen to me," I say.

"Oh, I know he won't." She gets up. "And if he fails?" She puts her hand on the door handle. "Quinn isn't the only one who will put a bullet in his ass."

I watch her walk out before I change out of my shorts into yoga pants and a tank top. When I walk out of the room, I'm met with silence. Walking to his bedroom, I see him on the bed trying to put a bandage on his leg.

"What happened?" I ask, and he looks up at me. I can tell that he's angry.

"Nothing," he says, his voice tight. I lean on the door and fold my arms over my chest. "Why are you still here?"

"I'm not sure you want to know the answer," I tell him honestly. He chuckles, and I know it's sarcastically as he shakes his head. "So I'm not going to answer you." He looks at me, shocked. I turn now, ignoring the pain in my chest as I walk over to the kitchen.

I wash my hands, looking out, and I see a couple of cowboys in the far distance as they put up something. Turning, I grab my baking stuff and get to work. "What the fuck are you doing?"

I look up now as I knead the dough I started. "I'm baking," I say. "It calms me." He watches my hands rolling the dough forward and then bringing it back. "When I was fourteen or fifteen, I used to go shooting when I got upset or pissed off."

"Why did you stop?" he asks, folding his hands in front of him on the island.

"I kind of"—I shrug—"sort of shot Quinn." He laughs, shaking his head. "It was a graze. But he got all 'you shot me.' He didn't even need stitches, and it barely bled." I roll my eyes. "So my parents took away my guns, and every time I got angry, they sent me to my grandmother's house. And it just stuck. Every single time I would get angry or annoyed, I would go on over, and she would teach me a recipe."

"What are you making?" he asks.

"Chicken and dumplings," I answer him. "Then I was thinking of some chicken potpie."

"Will you be making apple pie?" I look over at him.

"I may be persuaded to," I tell him. "Was Quinn okay with you?"

"He knows about..." he starts to say and taps the counter with his finger.

"He knows what?" I ask, not sure what he means. My mouth runs dry.

"That," he starts. "Apparently, you used to." He looks down, not sure of what to say.

"Follow you around." I laugh and make the dough into a round ball.

"He mentioned you following me to the barn." I look up at him.

"And I was trying to be all sly and shit." Turning now and grabbing a bowl, I place the ball of dough inside to rise.

"I remember," he says to me silently. "That day."

I look over at him, shocked he remembers that day. "What?" I ask.

"It was two years ago." He starts to talk now, and I don't move from my spot. "I hadn't seen you in over a year, and then you just showed up."

"I didn't just show up. Amelia picked me up at school." I wash my hands and then turn to look at him, and just like that day, he makes my heart speed up and my belly flip and flop.

"You got out of the car, and the wind picked up your hair a bit." He leans back in the chair. "You were wearing blue jeans and a white T-shirt tied at your stomach."

"I went to hug my grandfather, and I saw you walking away from the party," I tell him. "It took me over ten minutes to finally pry myself to the stable."

He gets up now and comes around the island to stand in front of me. "I was sitting in the barn with my head hanging down, telling myself you were perfectly wrong for me." He takes one of the strands of hair that's fallen out of my ponytail and wraps it around his finger. "You deserved to have someone who didn't have a house full of skeletons. You didn't deserve a broken man."

"I went into that barn." I put my hands on his hips. "Because I wanted to see if it was all in my head," I say, looking down. "I wanted to see if it was just a stupid schoolgirl crush." I swallow. "I wanted to see if you were everything my head remembered." He shakes his head. "I walked in and saw you sitting there, and you looked up at me." My hand goes to the middle of his chest, making sure that this moment affects him as much as it does me.

"You took my breath away." His voice is but a whisper.

I blink away the tears. "You were sitting there, and you were so much more than I remembered," I say. "My heart was going so fast when I saw you look over at me. I tried to act cool, but all I wanted was to walk up to you and kiss you. I wanted to feel what it would have been like to kiss you."

"I looked at you, and I wondered what it would be like to kiss you." He comes closer. "I wondered what it would be like to hold your hand." His hands cup my cheeks. "I wondered all this, and then the truth would come over me. The truth that you were perfect and so fucking wrong for me."

"But what if I'm not?" I ask. "What if I'm not wrong for you?" He shakes his head, and I know if I don't take this chance with him, I'm going to regret it for the rest of my life. "What if I'm the right one for you?"

"Chelsea," he says, almost as if he's pleading with me to stop talking.

"Mayson, you are a man with honor." My hand feels his heart beating, matching mine. "You are respectful. You are kind. You are funny." He looks at me with his eyebrows pulled together. "In your own way. You sacrifice yourself without thinking twice about it."

"You can stop now," he says, his breath hitting my face.

"Those," I say, "are the reasons I have fallen in love with you." He gasps. "You don't have to say it back. I don't expect you to say it back. If I've learned anything in the past couple of weeks, it's that tomorrow is not guaranteed. There is no time to tell you how much I love you." My hand moves up now from his chest to his face. My thumb rubs underneath his chin. "When you showed up, I was so scared to touch you." I swallow, ready to give him everything. "So scared I wouldn't be able to save you." One tear escapes now, and I bend to have it drop on the floor. "So scared I would be the one who couldn't save you and you would die before I got a chance to tell you that you, Mayson Carey, you are perfect."

"Chelsea," he says. "You don't mean it."

"I mean every single word, Mayson. I mean it from the bottom of my heart to the tips of my fingers." I turn my head to the side and look up at him. "And I'll remind you of this every single day that you let me." I swallow now. "Let me love you, Mayson."

I don't wait for him to answer me. I just inch my way closer to his lips. "I love you," I say softly, and then my lips fall onto his. I close my eyes and just feel him all over me. His tongue slips into my mouth as my hand goes to the back of his neck.

"Chelsea," he says as he moves his head from one side to the other. "I've dreamed of this moment," he says. "I've dreamed of kissing you." He kisses me so softly it feels like a dream. "Every single day."

"I'm here," I say, and one of his arms wraps around my waist. "I'm always here." His mouth falls on mine again.

"So wrong," he says between giving me kisses. "So fucking wrong." His hands cup my face, not letting me go. "So perfectly fucking wrong."

"Or," I say, my tongue sliding across his lower lip. "Or perfectly right."

Nineteen

MAYSON

"**P**erfectly right." Her voice is strong, and she never wavers. I push her hair behind her ears. "You need to stop," I say, and she shakes her head.

"You need to listen to me." She holds my face, leaning in to kiss me. The fear that was in her eyes when she got here is now gone. "I'm not going anywhere, and neither are my feelings."

Her hands go from my cheeks now to my lips. "Trust me."

"No one," I say, my hand going to rub her face like she is rubbing mine, I look into her eyes as I say the next part. "No one has ever said that to me before," I say another secret that I've never shared with anyone. "Not even my mother."

She blinks away tears as she looks at me. "She loved you." She smiles at me, and she furiously blinks away tears. "How can she not? Look at how perfect you turned out to be."

"Chelsea." Her name is on my lips all the time lately.

"Don't you dare," she says, leaning in and kissing me, and my heart fills for a whole different reason. "Don't you dare say anything."

"Will you let me even if I wanted to?" I lean forward and kiss her jaw.

"No," she says, and the timer rings. "Do you want to help me cook? Maybe it'll be a stress release."

I swallow, and I don't tell her that her in my arms is the only stress release I need right now. I don't tell her that just kissing her makes everything better. I tell her none of that because she deserves better than me, no matter what she says. "Sure," I say, and she steps away from me, going to the fridge and grabbing stuff. "What are we going to do first?"

"Well, one, wash your hands." She points at the sink and laughs. "God, I just sounded like my grandmother."

Walking over to the sink, I wash my hands and turn around to see her at the stove. "How are your cutting skills?"

"It's okay, I guess. I'm used to just cooking for myself," I say. "I've never complained."

"Okay, chop this." She puts the celery and an onion in front of me. She turns and walks over to the pot, putting the chicken in the water to cook.

"What is your favorite thing to eat?" She grabs another bowl and starts to cut apples.

"I don't think I have a favorite," I say. "When we are away, our food is usually bland and in a bag."

"There has to be something you would eat every day if you could." I swallow because I'm pretty sure I know the answer to that, and I am also pretty sure I shouldn't tell her.

"I guess I'm more meat and potatoes than fish and rice," I say.

"Well, then I'll stick to meat and potatoes," she says from next to me. I look over at her. "What?" She looks over at me.

"You," I just say. "You would do that, wouldn't you?" I ask, and she looks at me, confused. "Cook meat and potatoes every day if that is what I wanted."

"Well..." She shrugs. "I like that, too. So technically, I would be cooking it for myself. But..." She smirks. "I do a mean maple-glazed salmon."

I don't say anything else to her because I can't. Just the thought of having dinner with her every night is too much for me. I don't have time to get sidetracked with her. I can't go there, knowing that at any minute it could be taken away from me.

She shows me step by step what she is doing, and she helps me make the dough for the apple pie. "All you have to do is knead it." She puts her hands on mine as she shows me. Our fingers link with each other. "Gently," she says. She looks up at me, and everything I told myself is out the window. Her eyes sparkle as she looks at me, and her smile fills her face, making her even more breathtaking.

"Your eyes," she says. "Your eyes go darker when you look at me." I swallow down that she knew this, that she took the time to get to know all the little parts about me. "But they are the darkest when you come close and right before you kiss me." She leans in now and kisses me ever so softly.

I stand with her in the kitchen the whole time, and when she walks away from me, I follow her. I want to pretend I'm following her to learn, but I'm following her just to be next to her. Her hands graze mine sometimes, and then she moves around me by holding my hips, and my cock is just going to explode at this point. "It smells so good," I say, watching her wash all the pots while I dry next to her.

"Why don't you take a shower?" she says, handing me the last pot before turning off the water. "Then we can eat when you come out."

"Yeah," I say and put the pot down. "That sounds good." I lean down and kiss her on the lips, and I want to kick myself for just blatantly doing that. But the smile on her face makes me forget everything.

I walk over to the bedroom and take a shower as hot as I can stand it and then as cold as I can tolerate it. I ignore all the warnings shooting off in my head, telling me to just stop whatever this is. I can't think about her in that way. She doesn't need the shit I have in my closet.

I slip on a pair of boxers and sweatpants and a long-sleeved shirt. Walking out, I stop when I hear the soft music playing. The shades are all closed, and the lights are dim, and the table looks like she just set it. I watch her move around the kitchen and see she has changed. Her hair is loose, and she is wearing green pants that are loose but tight at the ankles. She wears a long-sleeved white shirt, and when she looks over at me, I see that one of her shoulders is bare. "It's done." She smiles as she bends and takes the potpie out of the oven. I walk over to her, and I can smell her citrus smell. If I could, I would lean down and kiss her shoulder, but instead, I just think about it. "You look handsome," she says, smiling, and all the words are stuck in my throat. All. Of. Them.

She walks over to the dining room and places the pie in the middle of the table. "Do you want a beer?"

"No." I shake my head. "I'm going to stick to water."

She walks back to the fridge and takes out the jug of water and another one of sweet tea. "I didn't make a side."

"The potpie is enough, Chelsea," I say, and she smiles at me. When I get really, really close to her, she looks up at me. Don't kiss her, don't touch her, my head is screaming at me. "You look beautiful," I say, putting one hand on her hip and then bending to kiss her lips.

"Thank you." She smiles shyly and sits down in the chair. I only sit when she does. She grabs my plate and scoops out some chicken potpie. She then serves herself half the portion.

"Do you say grace?" she asks, and I just shake my head.

"Do you?" I ask, and she avoids my eyes. "We can if you want."

"I usually just..." She avoids my eyes, and it kills me that she is afraid to tell me something. I put my hand on hers, and she looks at me from the side. "Thank you for keeping Mayson safe," she says and then mumbles, "Amen."

I take my hand off hers and grab the fork. The minute the food touches my tongue, I moan. "This is so good."

"Doesn't it taste a bit better knowing that you cooked it?" she asks me and I laugh.

"Let's be real, you tolerated me," I say, and I just look at her. "It was one of the best days in a long, long time. Being with you," I say before I can stop myself. But now that it's out there, how do I take it back? Better yet, I don't want to take it back. "I shouldn't have said that."

"Why?" she asks, avoiding my eyes, and it kills me that I made her sad. It kills me that anyone can make her sad, but most of all, that it was me. But my girl doesn't avoid anything. Instead, she folds her arms on the table in front of her, and she stares at me. "Why shouldn't you have said that? Is it because you don't mean it?"

"No," I say, shaking my head. "Not at all. I do mean it. I mean every single word," I say, and my hand cups her cheek. My thumb rubs her cheekbone. "I just meant that."

"Eat before it gets cold." I nod and finish my plate. She gets up and grabs the empty plate. I look up at her, and she kisses me so naturally, it's as if I've been doing it my whole life.

"Do you want ice cream with your apple pie?" she asks, and I get up and walk to her as she cuts the apple pie. She places a piece on the only plate on the counter.

"Are you not having any?" I ask, my mouth watering even though I'm stuffed. She shakes her head. "We can share," I say, and she gets the ice cream, digging one scoop out and placing it on top of the hot pie.

We stand in the middle of her kitchen at the counter, and she walks over and gets two spoons. "You go first," she says, and I cut into it, the ice cream melting into the piece. I take the piece and put it on my tongue, and the heat from the pie with the cool of the ice cream makes me close my eyes.

"If you ever think about another career," I say, taking another spoonful and now holding it up for her to taste. "You should think about becoming a chef."

She laughs, taking the apple pie from my spoon, and I pull it out too fast and a drop of ice cream remains on the corner of her mouth. I bend down to catch the drop with my tongue. She wraps her arms around my neck as my tongue slips into her mouth.

Dropping the spoon on the counter, I thread my fingers into her hair, pulling her even closer to me. We get lost in the kiss. Her hands going from my neck to my face, making sure the kiss doesn't stop. Her chest molds to mine, and I want to pick her up and carry her over to the couch. I want to lie with her and get lost in all the kisses she'll give me.

"Chelsea," I whisper and look at her as her eyes flutter open. The blue is now just a touch darker. Our chests rise and fall in unison. "I have never wanted anything in this world the way I want you," I admit. "Nothing and no one."

"Good." She smiles. "The feeling is mutual." I look down now, knowing that's all we can have. But I also know that I've never let myself have what I want in my whole life. "You should get to bed," she says to me as if she senses my turmoil.

"I think that is a good idea," I say, and neither of us moves.

"What do you want, Mayson?" she asks. "What do you really really want?"

All the words come to me and all the reasons also. But what comes out next shocks us both. "You." Her breath hitches as my heart hammers in my chest so hard and so loud. I think it's going to come out of my chest. "I want you."

Twenty

CHELSEA

I hold my breath as he fights with his inner demons. I can tell in his eyes how conflicted he is. I can also tell he's never ever put himself first. "What do you want, Mayson?" I ask, knowing that I shouldn't push him, and I've already pushed him out of his comfort zone. "What do you really really want?"

I'm expecting him to push me away, but what he says makes me gasp. "You." His eyes are so unsure. "I want you."

I walk to him, putting my hands on his face and feeling him. "Then have me," I whisper. His arms fly around my waist, and he moves his hand into my hair. His tongue slips into my mouth, and I get lost in him.

"I want," he says as he trails the kisses from my lips to my chin. "I want to pick you up and carry you to the couch."

"How about," I say, my eyes are still closed as he kisses me, "we walk over to the couch?" I turn in his arms and slip my hand in his as I drag him to the couch, sitting down and pulling him next to me. "I know you are almost healed, but I don't want to hurt you," I say, and he pulls me to him.

"You won't hurt me," he says, his voice gruff as he buries his hand in my hair and kisses me again. We kiss until we are both breathless. "We should get to bed," he says, and I lean in, kissing his neck. He gets up now and holds out his hand to me. I slip my hand in his and turn to walk over to the hallway. "Good night, Chelsea," he says, leaning down and kissing my lips. "Sweet dreams."

Turning, I walk to my bedroom, and I miss him. I wish he would have followed me to my room. I slip into bed and look toward the hallway. The minutes turn into over two hours, and I finally get up to make myself some tea. I try not to make noise, but when I walk out of my bedroom, I find him lying on the couch, looking out the window at the stars. "What are you doing here?" I ask, and he looks over at me.

"I couldn't sleep," he says. "So I thought I would look at the stars and try to see the beauty in them." My heart speeds up in my chest, and my stomach flutters.

I smile, walking over to the couch. "And?"

"The only thing I could think of was you." He reaches up and grabs my hand, pulling me down to him. I try not to squish him. "Lie with me," he says, and I don't answer him because I can't. The lump in my throat threatens to come out like a sob, and he might freak out. Instead, I lie on the couch with my back to his chest as he wraps his arms around me. We don't say anything as we both look at the stars, and it takes me less than ten minutes to finally fall asleep.

My eyes flutter open when I feel him move behind me. "Am I hurting you?" I jump up, afraid I've hurt him.

"No." He shakes his head. "I was trying to," he says and stops.

"What?" I ask, looking him up and down to make sure he's okay.

He looks down, almost as if he doesn't want to tell me. "I was trying to place my hard-on down."

My eyes suddenly fly to his cock, and I can see he's definitely up. "I didn't want you to wake up and have it poking in your back."

"Um," I say, and my cheeks blush now. "I'll make coffee," I say, ignoring his eyes. He gets up from the couch, and I hear him walking to his bedroom. Looking over, I see it is almost five thirty in the morning. When he comes out of his bedroom, I say, "I made you coffee."

He takes the cup from me and then turns. "Let's sit outside," he says, and we walk out to sit outside on the stairs.

"I'm sorry," he says, and I look over at him, the coffee cup at my lips. "About before. It was—"

"If you say it was a mistake." I shake my head, taking a gulp of the hot coffee and burning my mouth. "That is going to be a hard one to swallow." I laugh now. "Get it? Hard one."

He shakes his head and looks down. "I meant I didn't mean to disrespect you like that."

"I've never been with anyone," I finally tell him, my head telling me not to say anything and my heart holding on for dear life. "Like I've dated guys, but..."

"Are you saying...?" he says, and I feel suddenly so dumb.

"My mother was known as the town slut," I say and blink away the tears. "I mean, not now, but when she had Ethan." I swallow down. "Shit went down, and I don't really know the whole story because frankly, it doesn't matter. My mother is amazing. She is kind, she is loving, she is selfless when it comes to the people she loves and us." I look up at the sky as it starts to turn colors now. "She's been with my father for over twenty years, and people still talk about her. Less than before, but you would hear whispers even when I was in school." I wipe away the tear coming down my cheek. "So I wasn't going to give them anything more to talk about. I was going to show them that my mother raised a lady. That she wasn't what those people said she was." He wraps his hand around my shoulders and pulls me to him, kissing my head. "So you may think that we have this amazing family. And we do. But every family has some cracks in the foundation. It's about finding the crack and sealing it shut."

He doesn't say anything. We just sit and stare at the colors that fill the sky. We finish our coffee and walk in with the empty cups just as the door swings open, and Ethan walks in.

He stops in his tracks and smirks at Mayson. "You ready to hunt?" he says, and my stomach falls to the floor.

"Fucking right, I am," Mayson says without missing a beat. He walks to the bedroom.

"What's going on?" I ask Ethan, trying to control the beating of my heart. I don't even blink when Mayson is back and dressed in camo pants and a black T-shirt. The tattoo on his arm sticks out so much, or maybe I'm just focusing more on it.

"We are going to the base and share what we found out," Ethan says, looking at Mayson. He walks over to him and slaps his shoulder. "You look skinny."

"Fuck you," Mayson says, pushing Ethan away.

"Okay, let's go," Ethan says, and I stand here with my heart in my throat.

"I'm not leaving her alone," Mayson says, stopping Ethan in his tracks.

"Quinn is on his way," Ethan says, and I'm both annoyed and a little pissed but mostly sad he's leaving.

"I don't need a babysitter," I say, turning and not looking at either of them. "I have plans today anyway," I say, walking into the kitchen. "Have fun hunting," I say over my shoulder and walk to my bedroom. I make it to the bed before I hear the front door slam shut.

I don't move from my bed, and I don't know why I think he's going to come back and kiss me goodbye and tell me everything is okay. Deep down in my heart, I just know I'll never have him.

I ignore the pain in my chest while I get changed into my jean shorts that show off my lean, toned legs and a white short tank top that molds to my chest and falls just about my belly button. I slip on flip-flops, and I'm walking out the door when Quinn arrives.

"Where are you going?" he asks from inside his truck.

"Home," I say.

"Get in. I'll drive you," he says, and I know that I can argue with him and take my car, but he'll only end up following me there, and then my father will be all over him for not looking out for me. Instead, I just open the truck door and get in.

"Someone done pissed you off," he says, pulling away from my house.

"Why do you say that?" I look over at him.

"You just got in without arguing with me, so you are either fucking pissed or you're angry." He smirks at me, and I roll my eyes at him. "I'll shut up now."

"That would be smart of you," I say, looking out the window.

We pull up to the house that I grew up in, and we both just walk in. The smell of bacon and sausage fills the air. I dump my purse at the door, and when I walk into the kitchen, I find my mother just cleaning up. "Chelsea," she says, dropping the plate in her hand on the counter and coming over to me. She grabs me in her arms, and I don't know why, but I let go of the sob I've been holding. She's always been the one whose arms I've cried in. Always the one to hold me up when I couldn't hold myself up. It was a tough couple of years when Ethan left, and to be honest, we both had to hold each other up.

"I'll let you handle that one," Quinn says. "I'll be at the barn."

"Baby girl," she says in a whisper as she rubs down my hair.

"Are you hurt?" she asks, and I slowly slip out of her arms, rubbing away the tears with the back of my hand.

"I'm fine, Mom," I say. "It's nothing." I shake my head. "It's stupid actually, and I shouldn't have."

"Don't you ever apologize for the way you feel," she says. "Now, let's go sit outside, and you can fill me in on what I missed."

I grab a glass of sweet tea and walk out to the backyard. The sound of birds fills the air. "You haven't missed anything," I say.

"From what your father said," she says, sitting with me on the L-shaped couch they have outside right next to the fire pit. "You've have a rough couple of weeks."

I shake my head. "I wasn't the one who was shot."

"It took everything your father had not to rip you out of your own house," my mother says. "Me, on the other hand, I had different feelings about it."

"And what was that?" I ask.

"Oh, honey, please," she says, rolling her eyes now at me. "You have been in love with that boy for eight years." I just look at her, my mouth hanging open. "Who do you think you're talking to? If there is anyone who knows about loving someone from afar, it has to be me."

I laugh. "I thought I hid it so good."

"Oh, Jesus, anyone could take one look at you and know."

"Well, it doesn't matter," I say, sipping my tea. "The feeling is one-sided," I say and rub away a tear. "I was hoping that..."

"You were hoping that you would save him, and he would see how much you love him?" She puts the words into my mouth.

"I don't know what I was hoping," I say. "He thinks he can't be loved. He thinks I'm perfectly wrong for him." Saying the words out loud just cements what I was feeling. "He doesn't think he's worth it." My voice trembles as I think about how wrong he is.

"I know how that feels," my mother says. "To be from the opposite end of what everyone else is. To want so badly to be accepted but then be so scared that once you do, everything will be stripped away from you." She shakes her head now and wipes her own tear. "It's a fear I still have to this day." I look at her. "I love your father so much." She smiles through her tears. "And I know he loves me, but that fear lingers. Of course, it's less and less, and if you tell him this, I will deny it."

"He will never leave you," I say. "He would move heaven and earth for you."

"I know that," she says. "But..."

"I love him, Mom," I admit. "So fucking much that it hurts, and love isn't supposed to hurt like this."

"Oh, baby girl." She cups my face. "That is where you're wrong. The harder we love, the more it hurts."

"Yeah, well, I have to admit that I'm the only one on that street, and I don't want to be on it anymore." Saying it out loud is almost as if I'm admitting defeat.

"The heart wants what the heart wants," she says. "You can say what you want. You can vow to never look at him that way. You can even tell yourself that tomorrow you are going to wake up and not care." She smiles at me. "I lied to myself for eight years. Instead of the feelings going away, they just got stronger. They got even deeper and stronger."

"Well, that answers that question," I say, not sure I can handle it any more. "Good news is that once this is finished, he'll leave, so it might be a little easier."

She laughs. "Baby girl." She puts her arm around me. "Good luck with that."

Twenty-One

MAYSON

The door slamming shut makes my stomach sink down to my feet. I walk out of the house, and my feet feel as if my shoes are filled with concrete. Every step was harder and harder than the next. I sat with her and watched the sun come up while she poured her heart out to me, and all I did was walk out on her. I wanted to run back in and kiss her goodbye. I wanted to tell her all the things. But instead, I walked to the truck.

"You ready for this?" Ethan says when he puts his truck in park. I look up, seeing the massive white barn in front of me.

"As ready as I'll ever be," I say as I get out of the truck. I put my head down, and all I can do is think back to how I left Chelsea. A burning forms in my stomach and rises to my chest.

We walk into the cool barn, and I look at the five white desks in front of another wall. "Are you ready to have your mind blown?" Ethan says, walking to another door and putting his fingerprint on it. The door unlocks, and he walks in. I follow him, and I'm in shock.

The whole back wall is filled with five big screens side by

side. Five desks on each side of the room with full computers on it. "This looks like a military base."

"My uncle can be a little over the top," Ethan says to me. A side door opens, and Casey walks into the room with Jacob and Beau.

"Welcome to my playpen," Casey says with a smirk, and I shake my head.

"I thought he was a cowboy?" I mumble to Ethan, who just laughs now. "What is this place?"

"This is the eyes and ears of this town," Jacob says. "Along with a couple of other things that I can't talk about." He smirks at me.

"Let's get to work," Casey says from the big desk in front of the wall of five screens.

He's about to press something when the door behind us opens, and Quinn walks in. "What the fuck are you doing here?" I say, and he just glares at me. "You're supposed to be with Chelsea."

"She's fine. She's with my aunt," he says, looking at the guys. "I don't know what happened this morning"—he stares straight at me—"but she was pissed."

"Probably just because we got her a babysitter," Ethan says, and I let out a little sigh of relief that he is not questioning it. But I can't help but think there's something more to it, and I know that sooner rather than later, I'm going to be face-to-face with Quinn again.

"Mayson," Ethan says, and I turn to look at the screen in the middle. The picture is of my father right outside the diner. It's blurry, but you can tell it's him. "Is this your father?"

"It is," I answer him, rage now filling me. I spot Chelsea coming out of the diner and then the look on her face. It was so much worse than it was when she came home, and that was a look I would never forget.

We also spot him taking off for the bushes. "He knew what he was doing," I say out loud and sit down in one of the chairs.

"That's our thought, too," Jacob says. "We checked out the path he made, and a car's tire tracks were in the grass."

"Two people?" I say, and Casey nods.

"Two people?" I ask, shocked. "Who the fuck is he working with? Who would work with him? He was alone when he got me."

"How can you be sure?" Quinn asks. "You were tied to a fucking tree. He could have had ten people there, and you wouldn't know."

"I watched him come and go, and he did it by himself," I say.

"Okay, well, now that we have identified him," Beau says. "We can be on the lookout."

"From the looks of it, he's not in town." Jacob joins in now.

"How can you be so sure of that?" I ask, my mouth so dry I can't even swallow. "He could be hiding out somewhere right under our noses. Laughing at us."

"This town is small," Beau says. "If he was here, we would know."

"Not if he doesn't want you to," I say. "He was right in front of the diner. He was sending me a message."

"That is clear as day," Ethan says, and he leans back against the desk behind him.

"Now comes the tricky part," Casey says and types something on the table.

"Meet Braxton Michaels," he says, and a driver's license comes up, and it's my father. "This picture is from eight years ago."

"Fuck me," I say, and he pulls up all the credit cards that are owed. "How much is it?"

"Close to fifty," he says, and I think I'm going to throw up.

"Two years ago, things changed. His second wife died, and his funding ran out."

"What the fuck does that mean?" I ask, confused.

"It means that he tapped out of every option. All the cards were canceled." He looks at me. "The woman he married had SSI benefits, but when she died, so did the benefits."

"You mean when he beat her to death?" I hiss out, putting my head back and looking up at the ceiling. "Everything is just one giant clusterfuck."

"The good news is we have a paper trail," Jacob says.

"Now what?" I ask.

"Now the fun starts." Casey rubs his hands together. "I got you a house. Put your name on the mortgage."

I look at him, shocked. "What the hell for?"

"Because he's going to come back," Quinn says. "If he's the way you said he is, this motherfucker isn't going to be giving up until you stop breathing."

"We agree on one thing," I say.

"You live your life," Ethan says. "Go out. We give you a job."

"So you dangle me like a piece of meat." I fold my arms over my chest. The rage in me is making my arms shake. "How about we follow him? How about we find out where he is, and then I go there and put a fucking bullet between his eyes?"

"Now you have a plan, too," Jacob says. "Come to work here and see if you can find anything else."

"I have no other option," I say. "My back is literally to the wall."

Casey walks toward me and holds out a key. "This is the key to your place." He dangles the gold key in front of me. My hand extends to take it, and it feels like it's burning a hole in my palm.

"I'll take you back to Chelsea's, and you can get your things," Ethan says, and I just nod.

"I know it's a lot to take in," Beau says. "If it helps, my father was no father of the year."

I don't say anything. Instead, I just look at Ethan, and we both walk out. My head spins a mile a minute. I get into the truck and put my head back on the seat. "How're you doing?"

"Peachy," I say sarcastically.

"Just think of this as a mission," Ethan says. "Just another mission."

"Every time I start a mission," I say, "I make a plan for after."

"So let's make you a plan," he says. "Where are you going to go after this is all done?"

I swallow now. "Haven't decided," I say. My heart is heavier in my chest than when my mother died. "I've never planted roots anywhere." I look out the window as we pull up to Chelsea's house. My palms are getting sweaty now. "I've always liked this town."

He smiles. "I wouldn't be upset if you decided to stay here when all this is over."

"You never know," I say with my hand on the handle.

"I'll be back tonight to take you out of here." He looks around. "Easier to move at night than in broad daylight."

"I'll be waiting," I say, getting out of the truck. I walk toward the door and then turn back to look at Ethan. "What is the code to the garage?"

"Zero five thirty-one," he says. "Her birthday."

"That's safe," I mumble, going to the keypad, and it opens once I put the last number in. I walk into the house and call her name. "Chelsea," I say with no answer.

Walking toward the kitchen, I stop and all I can see is her at the sink beside me. Leaning over and kissing her. I look over at the couch where I spent the night away listening to her breathing beside me. Where I held her in my arms and for the first time in my whole life, I felt this calmness settle over me.

Breathing didn't hurt anymore. My eyes saw the goodness in the stars instead of the darkness that usually took over. I kissed her softly when she mumbled in her sleep.

"Every family has some cracks in the foundation. It's about finding the crack and sealing it shut." I hear her voice in my head over and over again.

"You don't have cracks in your foundation," I say to myself, walking to the bedroom and grabbing the bag. Opening the bag, I start putting my things in. My hands are almost not moving.

"You have no foundation." I walk over to the bathroom now and look at myself in the mirror. "She is too good for you. Let her go."

Twenty-Two

CHELSEA

"I needed this." I look over at my grandmother's face forming into the biggest smile. She really isn't my blood grandmother, but she has never treated anyone as if they weren't her blood.

"I haven't seen you bake that much since you made the decision to become a nurse," she says, sitting down next to me. She looks over at me. "what's got your panties in a bunch?"

"Not much," I answer quickly. "I start working for the clinic in a couple of weeks, and I guess I'm more nervous than I thought."

She puts her hand on mine. "Oh, honey, your gonna have them eating out of your hand.."

I smile at her and squeeze her hand in mine. The back door opens, and my grandfather comes in. He spots me sitting down and smiles, taking off his cowboy hat. "There she is," he says. I walk over to him, and he opens his arms for me. I wrap my arms around his waist just like I used to do when I was younger. He kisses the top of my head. "Missed you."

"Missed you, too," I say in his chest. "I smell pie," he says, letting me go, and I just laugh.

"We baked strawberry, blueberry, apple, and your favorite," Grandma says. "Pecan." She gets up and walks over to the stove to cut him a piece. "Come and have a little taste."

He walks over to her and bends to kiss her lips. Their love is one of a kind. The kind of love you wish for. The kind of love that survives the hard times. The kind of love I have wished for my whole life. "So what's troubling you?" Grandpa says, sitting down at the counter and looking over at me. "Twelve pies," he says. "Something must be weighing on your mind."

"Can't I just want to bake?" I throw up my hands. "Or that I missed Grandma."

"That," he says, pointing at me with his fork, "means someone has gotten under your skin."

"No one is anywhere," I say, walking to the fridge and grabbing the sweet tea. "Besides, if someone was under my skin, I'd be out shooting with you."

He chuckles. "You always had the best shot out of everyone," he says, and he is not wrong. He taught me how to shoot when I was almost twelve, and my aim was on point. He takes another bite. "How's your house guest?"

"Alive," I say, taking a sip of the tea. "Speaking of, I should get going."

"You coming on Sunday?" my grandfather asks, and I just nod my head. "You better or I'm going to come and get you."

"That is six days away," I say. "I'll be there."

"Good," he says. "Now let me finish my pie, and I can drive you home."

"I can walk," I say, putting my purse over my shoulder, and he just gives me the side-eye.

"You think just because I don't show up at the meetings with the men that I don't know what's going on," he says. "I know everything about my family. So let me finish this pie, and then I can take you."

"You can't argue with him, honey," my grandmother says, smirking at him. "Trust me, I've been doing that my whole life," she says.

"I let you win," he says, looking up as he takes his last bite, and my grandmother glares at him. "Like now, I'm going to let you win and kiss you right before I leave."

She shakes her head but lets him kiss her. "See you soon." She comes over to me and hugs me. "You come on back and cook with me whenever you have yourself in a pickle."

I shake my head and follow my grandfather out of the house. His pickup truck is the same one he's had for the past twenty years. Even though Uncle Casey bought him a new one five years ago, he still drives this one.

The door creaks when I open it, and when I sit down, I feel the springs under my butt. "It's time we retire this truck," I say. "Don't you think?"

"She still has a couple of years left in her," he says, and I laugh at him.

"You've been saying that for the last ten years," I remind him, and now he's the one laughing.

We pull up to my house, and I lean over the seat and kiss his cheek. "Thank you for driving me home," I say and open the door to get out. The creaking is even louder now, and I slam the door, and he watches me walk into the house.

I slip the key in and unlock the door, not sure if Mayson will even be back. The cool air of the house hits me right away as I step in, and my eyes go to the green duffel bag at the front door. The same bag Ethan brought him over last week. My heart starts to speed up in my chest even faster than it did this morning when he walked away from me. I put my keys down on the table in the front hall.

My hands are suddenly sweaty and shaking. I lock it down, blinking away the tears climbing into my eyes. With heavy feet,

I walk into the house, expecting him to be sitting on the couch waiting for me.

When I walk in and don't see him there, I go to the kitchen and take a glass out, walking over to the sink and filling it with some cold water. My mouth suddenly dry, my eyes are fixated on the trees outside.

I hear movement in his room, and I brace myself for what is coming. "Hi," he says, and I make the stupid mistake of looking over my shoulder and seeing him in jeans and a black shirt. His hair is still wet from the shower he must have just taken.

"Hi," I say, turning back around to look forward.

"Did you just get home?" he asks, and I nod my head.

"Yeah, Grandpa just dropped me off," I say, putting the glass in the sink and then turning around. "I'm going to go change." I avoid his eyes. I avoid even walking next to him. The lump in my throat is stuck when I get into my room, and I close the door. It's the first time I've done that with him in the house.

I slip into the shower, and I have to admit that I am stalling. I know he's leaving. I know that tonight when he goes to bed, it will be someplace else. I turn off the water right before the stinging starts in my eyes, and I avoid looking in the mirror. I slip on my shorts that have blue clouds on them and match it with a baby blue long-sleeved V-neck shirt. I look at myself in the mirror and see that my blue eyes shine even more with this shirt.

I walk out, and I somehow wish he had just left without talking to me. "Hey," he says again, and I honestly don't know what to do.

"Did you change your bandages?" I ask, walking to the kitchen and grabbing another glass. I need something in my hands so I don't just stand here and look at him.

"Can you look at me, please?" he says, his voice low, and I

take a deep breath and count to ten before looking up. I take a mental picture of him, but nothing beats him in real life.

"What is it?" I ask, standing in front of the island now, setting the glass down only because I'm afraid it will fall out of my hand and shatter.

"We need to talk," he says, and I laugh now.

"I'm pretty sure I know what you are going to say," I say. "I got the hint when I walked in and saw your bag at the door." I don't let him get a word in because I don't think I can handle the bullshit coming out of his mouth. "When are you leaving?"

"Tonight," he says. "It's easy to leave when it's dark."

I nod now, pretending I know what the fuck he's talking about. "Where are you going?" I want to kick myself. "Actually, you don't need to answer that."

"Your uncle got me a house," he says.

"Well, then, I guess everyone wins," I say, looking at him. He puts his hands on his hips, and his head hangs down.

"This morning..." he starts, but I put my hand up.

"Forgive me," I say. "For putting that on you." He looks at me, and I can see that his eyes have gotten darker. "If we can forget the past week happened." I swallow, but my mouth feels like it has a cotton ball in it. "We can just continue like..."

"Continue like you didn't tell me you love me?" he says, his voice getting louder. "Continue like I haven't had my lips on you? Continue like leaving this morning didn't kill me?"

"Well, you left and didn't look back, so we can go with that," I say, sounding hurt, and I want to kick myself.

"What the fuck was I supposed to say?" He looks at me. "Sorry, Ethan, I'll be right back. I just want to kiss your sister goodbye," he says, his voice calm. "Or maybe I could have said, Ethan, can you give me a second because I need to tell your sister that I can see what she means."

I look over at him. "What?"

"This morning," he says slowly. "Last night, I didn't sleep."

His eyes stare into mine. "The whole night you were in my arms, and I felt calm. I felt calm, and I felt at peace. I watched the stars all night long, and not once did I think of the darkness as evil. Not one time did I dread the next minute." I put my hand over my chest, hoping to calm down the beating. "Then this morning when we sat down and watched the sunrise, the same thing happened. I saw the fucking good. For once, I looked at the trees moving gently in the wind and thought it's a good day." He looks down now. "Then as soon as I felt that, your brother shows up." He shakes his head, looking down and then up again, and I see the anguish all over his face. "Then your brother shows up, and just like that, I'm reminded that there is no happiness for me."

Twenty-Three

MAYSON

I look down as my heart beats in my chest. I think my heart stops when I look up and see the pain in her eyes, but it's nothing like the pain I feel. "Then your brother shows up, and just like that, I'm reminded that there is no happiness for me." She looks down at her hands on the counter and rolls them around and around.

"Me here with you. Your kisses. Your touch. That is the happiest I think I could ever be." Might as well give it all to her. "Your smile." I look at her. "Your laugh, even your glare. Your touch." I close my eyes, pretending I'm close enough to touch her. Wishing I can do this with her in my arms. "Your kisses. Holding you in my arms. All of that makes me happy." My voice trembles now. "That is how I felt this morning walking out of here. But it was too good to be true. Because then there in black and white, I saw why I can't have it. Why I'll never ever get to have that happiness." My voice goes low with the last word.

"So I make you happy?" she asks.

"More than anything in the world," I say. "You have to

know that. You have to believe that." My stomach sinks with the thought of her not believing me.

She walks around the island now and comes over to me, sitting down at the far end of the couch. "Where are you going?" she asks with her hands in her lap as her foot moves up and down.

"Anywhere but fucking here," I say. "As far away from you that I can get." Her head snaps back as if I slapped her in the face. "I will not let you be in the middle of this. I will not have this fucking touch you. Don't you get that?" My hands are propped on my hips in anger now.

"No," she says, her voice cracking. "I don't get it." She gets up now. "But it's not my choice, now is it?"

"You think it's my choice?" I ask, and I want to run to her and pull her in my arms. I want to kiss her and push the hair away from her face.

"We all have choices." She stands there being so fucking strong. "And you chose to leave me behind."

"Me leaving will protect you!" I shout. "Don't you get that? Don't you see?"

"How?" she asks the loaded question. "You leaving me leaves me open for anything. Leaving me alone for him to just come in and..." She stops talking now.

The words hit me like ice water thrown on me in the middle of the desert. "He was here." I confirm to her that he was the one who creeped her out. "He was fucking watching you." The burning in my stomach is now coming full force.

"So, he knows I'm involved in this?" she says, and I want to kick myself because she is right. "Is he still in town?"

"No," I answer. "At least, that is what they told me, but who knows."

"Well, then, I guess all the plans have been made," she says, turning to walk away from me.

"My father was fucking here!" I shout as I look up and rub

my hands over my head. She turns, and I can see the sadness in her eyes. I put that there, me, me and my words.

"Yeah." Her voice is but a whisper. "And now he's not. I'm going to go lie down." She starts to walk away, and I can see the tears in her eyes.

"I'm talking about my father. The man who killed my mother," I say and see her face not even flinch when I mention him. "I'm talking about my father, who used my name to rack up tens of thousands of dollars in credit card debt." She doesn't say anything, and it's a good thing because I'm not finished. "I'm talking about my father, who married another woman and then beat her to death." I don't stop even though I know I should. "I'm talking about my father, who tied me to a fucking tree and tortured me for five days." I ignore the tear running down my face and the tears running down her face. "So that is why I'm fucking leaving you."

"You leaving won't change any of that." She walks over to me and stands right in front of me—my beautiful strong woman. I turn my head so the pain of looking at her will go away, but she doesn't give me the out. She puts her hand on my cheek and turns my head to look at her. "You are not your father. Would you hit me?" Just the thought alone makes rage fill my body. "Would you hurt your child?" I've never imagined having a child. I never gave myself the hope I ever would. It was a dream I buried so deep and was afraid to even think it. "You are not your father."

"I would never ever hurt you," I say, my eyes staring into hers. "If anything happened to you because of me..." I swallow down the lump in my throat.

"Then don't go," she says. "Don't leave me."

I don't have time to say anything to her as the front door opens, and her hand drops from my face. She moves swiftly to the other side of the living room, and we both look over to see Ethan standing there watching us.

"What is going on here?" he asks, looking first at me and then at Chelsea. I watch his eyes, and I know he knows something is up. He just hasn't figured it out yet.

"Nothing," Chelsea says. "He was just telling me that his father was the one watching me." She folds her arms now over her chest. "And that he's leaving to go somewhere else."

"He's going to stay at the Los Angeles house," he says, and I hold up my hand.

"I'm not fucking leaving here to go to LA." I put my hands on my hips.

"No, not LA," Ethan says. "It's my uncle's house. My aunt Olivia decked it out like an LA house. Everyone hates going over there, and Uncle Casey refuses to tell her, so he just keeps it for visitors."

"I don't think that is a good idea," I say, and I'm shocked by my own words. "If I leave here, your sister is going to be left open."

"We'll have eyes on her," he says, and I shake my head.

"He'll come for her just to get to me," I admit. "He knows she helped me. He knows I was here. That's why he went after her before coming to get me."

"You really think he'll use her?" Ethan asks me.

"Without batting an eye," I answer honestly. "He will come to her to get to me. Just to fuck with me."

"Fuck," Ethan says, running his own hands through his hair. "Fuck, fuck, fuck."

"I hate to do this," I say now. "You have no idea how much I hate to put her in this."

"I'm already in it," Chelsea says. "So now that we've got that out of the way."

"Tomorrow," Ethan says. "You start living your life."

"Meaning?" Chelsea says, looking at both of us.

"Meaning you go do what you do during the day, and Mayson gets his ass into the barn, and we find his father before his father finds him." She puts her hand to her stomach. "I'm going to talk to Casey and Dad and make sure we have someone shadow you." He looks at me, and I nod. "Now I have to get home. I promised I would give the kids a bath. Call me if you need anything," he says, and the door slams shut.

"I hate this," I admit. "I hate all of this."

"I know that I should," she starts, "and I don't like your father at all. But…"

"But nothing." I shake my head now. "Don't even fucking say it."

"Will you promise me something?" She looks at me, and she wrings her hands.

"Anything," I say. I will give you anything, I say to myself only.

"That no matter what happens, you won't lie to me," she says. "That no matter what happens, if shit is going to be bad, you tell me it's going to be bad."

"It's going to be bad," I say. "It's going to be bad because I will not stop until I kill him." I watch her eyes watching me. "That is who you think you love."

"If it's a choice between you or him," she says without batting an eye. "There is not even a choice."

"I just told you I'm going to kill a man, and you didn't even bat an eye." I point at her.

"Is that why you said it?" she asks. "To see if I would be shocked. I give up," she says. "I give up." She walks now and stops in front of me. "I give up trying to get you to see what I see." She gets on her tippy-toes and kisses my lips softly.

My eyes watch her now as she walks away from me. "You are the most beautiful person I have ever met." She stops in her tracks, and I see her head hang down. "This morning when I left here, I felt like I had concrete in my shoes." She doesn't turn and look at me. But she moves her hand to her stomach. "From the moment I've seen you, you've been the woman I'm chasing in my dreams." I tell myself to shut up and just let her go, but something inside me just pushes forward. "Everything." I take a step forward, hoping she fucking turns around. "Everything was for you."

"How?" she says, turning around, and I see the tears running down her face. "How could leaving me be for me?" Her voice kills me. "How could you think that you leaving here would be for me?"

"Don't you get it?" I look at her. "Leaving you would save you." I take a deep breath. "It would have saved you." I walk over to her now, my heart beating so fast in my chest I look down to see if you could see it. I stop in front of her, so close to her. My hand comes up, and I wipe the lone tear that has just fallen over her bottom lip. "It would have destroyed me," I admit, my fingers touching her face. My fingers are shaking as I touch her. "Not being able to do this again," I admit. "To touch you." I trail her cheek and then move down to her jaw. "Even if just for a minute, it would have destroyed me."

Twenty-Four

CHELSEA

My whole body tingles when he touches me. "Chelsea," he says in almost a plea. "I won't survive if something happens to you."

"Are you staying?" I ask as his fingers touch my chin, and then he palms my face. His thumb rubs my bottom lip. "Are you staying here with me?"

I wait without breathing for his answer. "Yes," he says.

"Then I'll be safe," I say, putting my hands on his hips. "With you here, I'm safe."

"I don't think I can go back," he says, licking his lips. "I won't be able to go back and pretend you don't mean anything to me." I look down, and the tears are coming now as my body shakes. "Chelsea." He says my name again, and it's like music to my ears.

I look up at him and see he has his own tears in his eyes. "Don't," I finally say. "Don't go back." My hand comes up to cup his cheek. "I'm yours." I shrug one shoulder. "All of me is yours." I drop my hand and take the biggest risk of my life. "Make me yours." I hold out my hand now. "Make me all yours."

I slide my hand into his as I pull him toward my room. We walk into my bedroom, and I stand here in the middle of the room, right in front of the king-size bed that I picked out with the plush white carpet under my feet. I step up to him now as he looks around my room. A room I took my time picking things out for, secretly hoping for this moment right here. The whole back wall is white rustic wood. A wooden stepladder leans against the side wall with five blankets hanging from it. "I'm nervous," I admit, looking down, trying to calm my nerves down.

He shakes his head, coming to me, and when I look up at him, he pushes my hair behind my ears. "My palms are all sweaty," he admits and picks up one of my hands and places it on the middle of his chest. "I feel like my heart is going to rip through my chest." His heartbeat matches my own. "I'm afraid," he admits, his voice low. "I'm afraid I'm going to get a taste of you and then..." He looks down now, and his heartbeat speeds up. "I'm so afraid it'll be the happiest day of my life, and then in a blink of an eye, it'll be gone."

"Don't let me go," I say, and I'm secretly begging him to never let me go. "I'm not going anywhere," I let him know, and he puts his thumb on the side of my face. He leans his face down, and his lips hover over mine. My whole body shivers from his touch, my stomach flutters just knowing he's going to kiss me any minute. He turns his head to the side just a bit and slips his tongue into my mouth. My hand moves from the middle of his chest to wrap around his waist. I kiss him with everything I have. We kiss each other softly, our hands pushing ourselves even closer. My fingers roam from his hips to the hem of his T-shirt, slipping under it, and he lets go of my lips to put his head back. I lift his shirt now over his chest. I've seen and touched his chest before now, but something about touching him now makes my body come alive. "I don't want to hurt you," I say, my hands going to the bandage.

"You could never hurt me," he says. I bend forward and kiss him in the middle of his chest where his heart is beating erratically. "Chelsea," he whispers my name, and I turn, going to the bed.

"Will you lie with me?" I stand by the bed, waiting for him to come to me. He walks over and puts his knee on my bed and pulls me with him. He lies in the middle of the bed, and I get on the bed beside him. With my hand on his chest, he leans up and kisses my neck, sucking it. My hand roams as his kiss goes from my neck to my ear. I turn now as he takes my mouth again. The kiss is stronger than before as he turns us both on our sides now. Our chests are pressed together just for a minute before he puts me on my back. My legs open for him to fit between.

He lets go of my lips as he trails kisses all the way from my cheek to my neck, my back arches when I think he's going to cup my breast. I moan out in frustration when I can't feel his kisses anymore. My eyes flutter open as I look down at him, pulling up the shirt, and then he bends his head and kisses the side of my stomach. "Every single inch of you," he says, "is going to be kissed by me." My hand comes up and goes into his hair as he pulls the shirt higher. He moves his kisses to my ribs as his tongue slips out now and slowly licks all the way up. My nipples are already hard, waiting for him.

"Mayson," I pant out his name, my whole fucking body on edge. I just need to feel his skin on mine.

I need him to just rip my shirt off. He finally pushes it up, exposing my baby blue lace bra, which leaves nothing to the imagination. "Fuck," he hisses, cupping one of them while he bends to take the nipple in his mouth right through the lace.

I watch him move from one to the other and then slowly trace the top of my breast with his fingers before slipping them in and finally touching my nipple. He pushes the bra down and then slips his head down. Taking the nipple between his teeth, he bites softly, the pleasure shooting straight to my stomach and all the way to my core. "You're fucking perfect," he says, and my eyes close now as he moves from one nipple to the other. I'm on edge, and he hasn't even taken my shirt off.

"I need to feel you," I say, and he just looks at me. "Your skin on mine," I finally say and sit up, pulling my shirt over my head and grabbing the bra at the same time. I lean in, kissing his chest, and I see his stomach sink in a bit. My hands stop moving. "Is this okay?"

"It's more than okay," he says. "It's just," he starts to say. "I'm trying really hard not to," he says as my hands go from his chest to his neck, "lose control."

"Why?" I ask him.

"Because," he says softly. "I want to take my time with you. Savor you." He kisses my lips, his tongue sliding onto mine but with more need. I lie down, and he sinks onto me, his chest on mine. My legs wrap around his hips as my pussy lines up with his cock. I move my hips brazenly, and he lets go of my lips to hiss out.

"Did I hurt you?" I ask worriedly.

"No." He shakes his head. "But if you do that one more time, it's going to be really fucking embarrassing for one of us," he says. "I don't think I can wait much longer." He leans down, taking a nipple into his mouth, and then moves down the middle of my stomach to the hem of my shorts. "Tell me this is okay." He looks up at me.

"All of me," I say, "is yours." His fingers slowly pull my shorts down along with my lace thong, and I lie here fully naked in front of him. I lift my hand to cover one breast shyly and try to close my legs. "Don't," he says, his eyes turning almost black. "Don't hide from me." He gets lower now and moves his lips left and right across my stomach. "I have to taste you," he says. When his tongue licks up my slit, I feel like there are stars all around me. My hips move up on their own as he sucks in and then licks up again. My hands grip the sheets next to me as his tongue flicks my clit. My body is shaking, and I can't help but watch him eat me. When his eyes meet mine, he stops, and I'm the one who groans.

"Why?" I ask him.

"Because I want to kiss you," he says, moving from between my legs now. "I want to play with you," he says, and I just look at him as he leans down to kiss me. One hand cups his cheek, and the other hand goes to the back of his neck as I taste myself on his tongue. He is kissing me when I feel his fingers touch my pussy. He moves them up and down and then slips his two fingers in me. He swallows my moan now, his mouth never leaving mine as he plays with me. His fingers move faster and faster, and I can feel myself getting wetter and wetter. Our tongues are going around and around in circles as he takes me to the edge of the cliff. His thumb strums my clit back and forth, and I finally let go.

"Mayson." I let go of his lips, and he buries his face in my neck as his fingers never stop, and I come all over them. I pant, trying to open my eyes, but I can't. My whole body feels like a noodle as his fingers take me to the edge again and again. I close my legs on his hand, making sure he doesn't move.

"Perfect," he says, and I open my eyes, looking at him as he stares at me. My chest is heaving.

"That." I try to think of words. "That was." I shake my head. "I've never." I put my hand on his chest. "That was intense."

I sit up, the wetness from my pussy making the bed wet. "You are wearing too many clothes," I say, and he just looks at me as my hands go to the button on his jeans. "Can I touch you?" I ask, stopping to make sure it's okay.

"It's..." he starts to say. "I don't know if that's a good idea." My hand moves back now, and I'm afraid to touch him. "No, no," he says, pulling my hands to him. "It's just. Well." I look at him. "It's been over eight years." I stare at him now. "You weren't the only one," he says and then shakes his head. "What I mean is you weren't the only one with feelings. I couldn't get you out of my head." I look down, hiding my smile. "So I'm afraid that if you touch me, I'll have no control."

I get on my knees in front of him. "I'll be gentle," I say as I unsnap his button and pull down his zipper. His hard cock is filling the gap. "I'll be really gentle," I say to him.

"Great," he says sarcastically as I pull the jeans over his hips. "Just fucking great," he says through clenched teeth when I pull his boxers down and his cock springs free.

My hand moves without even thinking as I grab his thickness in my hand. I lean down and lick the tip of his cock. His hands go to my head, and I look up to see his head back with his eyes closed, and it gives me a power I didn't know I had. Just as he let me lose control, knowing I have the same power makes me take the tip of his cock in my mouth and taste the saltiness from his pre-cum when it hits my tongue. I take as much as I can of him down my throat before moving back up again. My hand moves with my mouth. I get to the tip, letting go and then licking around again in a circle. "Fuck," he says, his eyes watching me. I suck his cock and move my hand with my mouth. His eyes never leaving mine. I lick down the shaft, my hand wet from my mouth. "Okay, enough," he says. "I can't wait any longer." He looks into my eyes. "Lie back."

I get back in the middle of the bed and lie here with my legs spread for him. I watch him take off his pants, and then he suddenly stops moving. "What's the matter?"

He looks at me with the most pained look of his life. "I don't have a condom."

Twenty-Five

MAYSON

We are in the middle of her bed, both of us naked, when it finally dawns on me. "I don't have a condom." I mean, why the fuck would I need a condom? For the past eight years, I haven't looked at anyone else, so there was no point in carrying around a condom.

"I'm on the pill." She looks at me. "And I'm clean obviously, I've only ever." I put my hand up.

She leans over to the side table and reaches in, bringing out a silver dildo. "This is the only thing I've been with."

"Interesting," I say, taking it from her and tossing it over my shoulder, hoping that it shatters on the floor. "I'm clean," I say. I wait for her to say something else, but she doesn't. Instead, she lies back down in the middle of the bed and spreads her legs for me. If I thought she was hot with clothes on, nothing could have prepared me for seeing her naked. Her perfect plump tits fit perfectly in my hand. Her pussy has a small landing strip, and she tasted like a juicy strawberry in the middle of a summer day. I crawl between her legs, my cock in my hand, and I stroke it because if I don't, I'll probably come all over her without even getting into her. Her legs open wider for me, and when I'm close enough, I take my cock and slide it up and down her slit. She's just as wet as when my fingers were buried inside her. I move my cock up and down a couple of times and then put my cock at her entrance. I push forward just a touch, and the tip slowly slips into her. Her pussy is strangling my cock already. I have to close my eyes before I pound into her. I open them again, and she just looks at me. "Tell me if I hurt you."

"I need you," she says, wiggling her ass left and right. "I need you to move." Her hands reach out to her sides as she grips the covers in her hands. "More."

I pull out a bit and then slowly give her a bit more. I watch her face to make sure she isn't in pain. I continue moving in and out until I'm finally buried all the way in her with my balls slamming against her ass. Both of us are now moaning. "I need you not to move," I say as I feel her hips moving up and down.

"But," she says, and I lower myself on her. "But." She moves again right and left. "I need."

My forehead on hers, I cup her face in my hand. Her hands come up to grab both sides of my neck. Our eyes are locked to each other as I move my hips. "I love you," I say. "I don't know what love is," I say as I bury myself in her over and over again. "But this feeling." We both pant out. "I've never felt it before."

Her hips move with me. "I love you," she says. "From the first time I saw you." I kiss her, and I know she's close because her pussy gets even tighter, and I can barely pull out of her. "I was yours."

"Mine," I say to her as my thrusts get stronger and stronger. The sound of skin slapping fills the room. "Fucking mine," I say as she comes on my cock with my name on her lips.

"Yours," she says right before I plant myself balls deep in her and come inside her. I collapse on her chest and turn her to the side so I don't squash her. "That," she says, moving her nose along my chin. "Was—"

"The fucking best," I say, moving away from her so I can see her face. Her cheeks are flushed from her orgasms, her eyes crystal blue with happiness.

"Are you okay?" I ask, looking down and seeing that I'm still buried in her. My cock is softening but still not willing to come out of her.

"I'm fine," she says. "My vibrator." She looks toward the floor where it lies. "I'm not sure about that." We both laugh, and she cups my cheek. "Did you mean it?" I look at her. "When you said you love me."

"I don't know what love is," I say the truth, "but I know that when you walk in the room, my heart speeds up. I know that when I think of you, something fills me. I know that when you are next to me, all I want to do is hold your hand and kiss you. I know that it would kill me to see you hurt, and I know I would die for you."

"Isn't it beautiful?" she asks, smiling like she's never smiled before. "That feeling that just overwhelms you when you think of that other person."

I look at her now, and I understand exactly what she means. It's the overwhelming feeling that you can't control. "Yeah, it is." Rolling away from her, I get off the bed. "I'm going to start a bath."

"You can't take a bath," she says, getting up on her elbow. "Your stitches aren't healed yet."

"But you can," I say, and she gets off the bed.

"I want to take a shower," she says, walking away from me. "Then I'm going to get some pie." She looks over at me. "Are you just going to stand there?"

I shake my head, and we take a shower together. Our hands roam over each other. She gets out first, and I follow a couple of minutes later. I find her wearing a robe in the middle of the kitchen as she makes two plates of food. "Hey." She looks up, smiling at me, and I stand here in a towel. "I thought you might be hungry."

"I am." I walk to her and wrap my arms around her waist, and I kiss her neck. My cock is coming alive already with just one touch. We eat side by side, and I spend the whole night kissing every single part of her body.

Neither of us sleeps all night long. The need to touch each other proves to be stronger. She slides out of bed at five thirty, slipping her shorts on and the shirt she was wearing when she led me to her bed.

"Where are you going?" I ask, and she looks over her shoulder, smiling.

"I'm going to watch the sunrise," she says, walking out of the bedroom. I get up, slipping on a pair of shorts, and find her holding two cups of coffee.

"Morning," I say, grabbing my cup and kissing her lips. We walk outside and sit on the step, except this time, I do it with my arm around her back, with her as close to me as she can get. Neither of us says a word as I watch the colors, and for the first time in my life, I look at them the way she does.

I get up first, holding out my hand for her, and she takes it, leading me inside. "What do you want for breakfast?" she asks, walking over to the fridge.

"Your brother is on his way." She looks over at me. "I texted him last night." I don't have to say anything or better yet I can't because the front door opens and closes. "Right on time."

"Mayson," she whispers.

I just shake my head as he comes in and stops to look at us. "Hey," he says, looking from me to Chelsea. "Everything okay?"

"Yes," Chelsea says and walks around the island.

"I need to talk to you," I say, walking over to the living

room and trying to get away from Chelsea in case Ethan loses his mind and attacks me. I don't want her to get hurt in all this.

"Did you remember something?" he says, coming in and sitting on the couch across from me.

"Actually," I say. "This has nothing to do with my father. It has to do with me."

"Okay," he says, putting his elbows on his knees.

"I'm in love with Chelsea," I spit it right out, and I see his eyes start to open wide.

He sits up straight, looking at me, and then his eyes look at Chelsea, who is now standing in the middle of the hallway with her hand to her mouth, shaking. I'm out of my chair, rushing to her. "What's the matter?" I whisper to her as I take her in my arms. "Are you hurt?"

"No," she says. "It's just.

"You just..." she says, her voice shaking.

"What the fuck is going on here?" We both hear Ethan behind us. We turn now, and she slips her hand into mine. "You didn't even want him at your house." He looks at Chelsea, then looks at me. "You haven't said two words to her," he says, "since you've met."

"Eight years ago," I start, "I walked into your grandparents' picnic, and she was wearing blue jeans and a white T-shirt tied at the waist. She was on her horse, and she was laughing, the sight of her literally stopped me in my tracks. Then every single time I came, I would secretly hope I could see her." I shake my head now. "I know that I shouldn't have thought of her in that way out of respect to you. And I swear if..."

"The heart wants what the heart wants," Chelsea says, and I look at her. "That's what Mom told me."

"For fuck's sake, Chelsea," Ethan says.

"With all due respect," I say. "Don't talk to her like that."

Ethan just stares at me. "Excuse me?"

"Look, I get she's your sister, but you have to understand she's mine," I say. "I don't have anything to offer her. I have nothing." I look over at her. "I have the clothes on my back."

"You know I don't care about that," she says to me, then turns to Ethan. "I chose him," she says. "Out of every single person in this whole world." She squeezes my hand. "I want him."

He runs his hand through his hair. "Dad is going to fucking freak out," he says. "This is crazy." He shakes his head. "Your father is hunting you down, and now my sister is involved."

"I was involved the minute I opened the door." She steps forward now. "I'm not backing away from him because of his father. I don't care what you say or Dad says or what anyone says. I have loved this man for the past fucking eight years," she says. "Waiting, hoping that he would somehow see me as not just your little sister but a woman who wanted nothing more than for him to notice."

I noticed you," I say, pushing her hair behind her ear. "I noticed you. I noticed all of you."

Twenty-Six

CHELSEA

"I noticed you. I noticed all of you," he says softly, putting his arms around my waist and pulling me to him. My arms wrap around him, and I lay my head on his chest.

"This is not okay," Ethan says, shaking his head. "She knew." We both look at him. "Emily, she saw it. I told her she was crazy."

"She is not crazy," Mayson says.

"Now what?" Ethan looks at me.

"Now, I call Mom and go over there for dinner and tell them." I look over at Mayson, who just nods.

"I really hope you know what you're doing," Ethan says. "Now get dressed. We have work to do."

"Let me make breakfast," I say, walking over to the fridge. "He has to change his bandages anyway."

Mayson kisses my lips and walks to his bedroom. I turn now and look at Ethan. "Whatever you want to say," I say, "don't."

"If you get hurt," he says, his voice tight and low. "I will kill him myself." I've always known Ethan was cutthroat. He came back from the military, and with one look, he would have you backing out of the room. I look at him. "Without thinking twice."

"If anything happens to him." I point at the bedroom. "I don't know if I would survive," I say. "I love him. Like so much, the thought of him not being here is just." I shake my head and swallow down the lump in my throat. "I can't explain it." Even though I fight back the tears, they still come. "I can't lose him, not now that I have him."

"Why is she crying?" I hear Mayson hiss from behind me and turn to him.

"I'm not crying." I wipe my cheek with the palm of my hand. "I was just talking."

"She's fine," Ethan says, and I make them both breakfast. Ethan places his plate in the sink at the same time Mayson finishes. "You ready?"

"Yeah," Mayson says, getting up now and coming over to the sink.

"Let's go," Ethan says, and Mayson doesn't move this time.

"I'll be right out," he says to Ethan, and I just smile at him. "Come here, Chelsea."

I walk to him, wrapping my arms around his neck. "Will you be safe?" I ask, scared now that something is going to happen to him.

"I'll be fine," he says. "Give me a kiss." He doesn't have to ask me twice before my lips are on his. I don't stop kissing him until we hear the car horn blare, and we both laugh. "I have to go."

"You do," I say and then look down. "But I'm not sure if you want my brother to see you saluting." I wink at him and walk away. "I'll text you later." I walk into the bedroom and fix the bed.

Grabbing my phone, I call my mother, who answers after half a ring. "Chelsea," she says almost with a fear. "Are you okay?"

"I'm fine," I say, "but I was wondering if I could come over for dinner."

"Why the hell are you asking that?" my mother shrieks. "You don't have to ask to come over to your own house for dinner."

I laugh. "Okay, well, then, I can come over soon, and we can spend the day cooking together."

"Or I pick you up in thirty, and we can go get our nails done," she says, and I laugh. "See you soon, baby girl."

I toss the phone on the bed and slip on the baby pink T-shirt dress and grab my gold flip-flops. I tie my hair in a ponytail, and when my mother comes to get me, I walk out of the house with a smile. But then I feel someone watching me, and I stop and look around. My mother gets out and comes over to me. "You okay?" she asks, and I just nod.

"I'm fine, just felt eyes on me." I shake my head. "It's probably just in my head." I close the car door, and for the rest of the day, I forget about the feeling.

~

"ETHAN SAID HE'S GOING TO BE HERE IN TEN minutes," Emily says to us as she holds Aubrey in her arms. "Can you hold her? I need to go to the bathroom." She hands me my niece, who just smiles at me and lays her head down on my chest. "She didn't nap today, and if she goes down now." She shakes her head. "There will be no mommy daddy time."

I laugh at Emily as she walks away from me. I sit on the couch, kissing her head as she watches her cartoon on the television. The screen door slams shut, and I hear footsteps coming into the room. My father is the first one to walk in smiling when he sees me and then Aubrey.

Ethan and Mayson are right behind him. Aubrey sees Ethan and calls his name. "Da da da da." Holding out her arms, he comes over and takes her from me. "There is my princess," he says, kissing her head. "Where is Momma?"

"Bathroom," I say, and Mayson stands there next to my father with a weird look on his face. "Hey," I say to him and then get up to hug my father. My mother comes into the room, and my father walks to her and hugs her, kissing her lips.

I walk to Mayson, and I smile at him. "Hey there," I say, and I don't know if I should kiss him or not. I am not sure how we are going to do this. I've thought about it all day, and then I tried to tell my mother, no lie over a hundred times, but each time, I stopped talking.

"Hi," he says softly, and I just walk close to him and kiss his lips.

"Hi," I whisper, and we don't notice the silence in the room. I turn and see that everyone is looking at us. "Well," I say under my breath. "Here we go."

"What the fuck is going on?" my father says, putting his hands on his hips. He looks at me and then Mayson. Then he looks at Ethan, who is hiding his smile with Aubrey's head.

Emily walks back in the room, stopping when she senses something is wrong. "What happened?" she asks, looking around, and I slip my hand into Mayson's and smile at him.

"We're dating," I say to them.

"Called it," Emily says and stops talking when she looks over at my father, who is shaking his head.

"Absolutely fucking not," he says and my mother goes to his side and calls his name in a whisper. "Don't start with me, Savannah. This is not happening."

"Um, with all due respect, Dad," I say, "I'm twenty-three."

"I don't care if you're sixty," he says now. "This is not happening." He uses his finger to go between Mayson and me. "Chelsea, think about your future," he says, and I just look at him, shocked. "This is about what's at stake right now. Just last month, he was fighting for his life."

I'm about to grab my stuff and walk out of the house. "You can't just be in a relationship with him. He..." he starts. "He..." But he doesn't have a chance to finish because Mayson speaks.

"I know I'm not your first choice," Mayson says, and we both look over at him. "Trust me, if I had a daughter, I would not want her with someone like me. I can't give her what she needs, but I know that I will protect her and love her. I have nothing. I am nothing."

"You are everything," I say.

"Listen, I know that you have a lot going on right now." My father looks at Mayson.

"He's me," my mother says, and my father looks over at her. "Right now in that spot." She wipes the tears from her face. "He was me all those years ago."

"No, he's not," my father says.

"You are judging him because of who his family is," my mother says to my father, the tears just rolling off her cheeks. "You are doing to him what everyone did to me. We are a product of our environment. He is not his father, just as I am not my mother." She shakes her head.

"That is what everyone whispered about me every single time. That is what some of them still say about me." She looks at my father. "How many times did people tell you to walk away from me?" My father doesn't say anything. "I loved you from afar all those years because I always felt I was nothing."

"Mom," Ethan says, and she looks over at him.

"I feel what he just said." She looks at the whole room. "I felt it deep down to my bones. Knowing that you love this person, yet everyone thinks you aren't good enough for him. That I wasn't good enough for you." She looks at my father. "Would you have walked away from me?"

"You know that I wouldn't," he says, walking to her.

"Then don't expect your daughter to," she says and bends her head. My father takes her in his arms and kisses her head. She turns and looks over at me, and I have my own tears running down my face. I look over at Emily, who just stands next to Ethan as she kisses his arm.

I look up at Mayson, who just wraps his arm around me and kisses my head as I wrap my arms around his waist. "I'm sorry," my mother says, looking at Mayson. "We taught our kids to accept everyone no matter who they are or where they come from." She looks at my father. "My husband tends to forget sometimes."

"I just don't want her to get hurt," my father says.

"We are on the same side," Mayson says. "I tried to fight it."

"The heart wants what the heart wants," my mother says, and Ethan and my father both groan. "Excuse me?" she says, putting her hands on her hips. "Did you guys just groan at me?"

"Here we go," Emily says, and Mayson looks at me now.

Ethan and my father start trying to talk to my mother, who ignores them and walks out of the room. "You." My father points at Ethan. "This is your fault."

"You groaned with me," he tells him. "I think your groan was even louder than mine."

My father shakes his head as we hear cupboards in the kitchen slam shut. "She's pissed," Emily says, grabbing Aubrey from Ethan. "Which means you guys go in that kitchen and say you're sorry."

"Fuck," my father says, running his hands through his hair. "Baby," he says, calling to my mother as he walks out of the room. "I'm sorry."

"I don't have much experience in this," Mayson says low. "But what the fuck just happened?"

"You just experienced your first family talk," Emily says,

"and then a family fight." She smiles at him. "You got a twofer." She kisses her daughter's head. "Welcome to the family."

The front door opens again, and this time, Gabriel comes running in. "Mom, Dad," he says, ignoring us. "Uncle Toby and Uncle Keith taught me how to shoot a gun."

"Oh, here we go," I say, and Mayson just looks at me. "Family fight number two coming in three, two, one," I say, and we hear the front door slam again.

Twenty-Seven

MAYSON

I turn her over and lick from her stomach up to her neck as her chest rises and falls in deep pants. "I need just..." she says softly, picking up her arm, and then it drops with a plop on the bed next to her. I suck on her neck, and she moans. "Mayson." Her hips are rising now.

I rub my cock up and down her slit, sliding in easily. I close my eyes for just a second as her pussy squeezes the shit out of me. Her hand goes to my ass to make sure I don't move. "Not fair," she says breathlessly. "You said I could ride you."

I smirk down at her and kiss her lips. "If my girl wants to ride me..." I slip out of her, and she groans. "Then she is going to ride me." When we got home from dinner with her parents, we lay on the couch, and it was only minutes before we were both naked, and she rode me for the first time.

Now, it's twelve hours later, and she wants to ride me again. I sit in the middle of the bed as she throws a leg over my hips. Grabbing my cock, she slides down it. "Yes," she whispers, wrapping her hand around my neck. Looking up at her, I see that her cheeks are flushed and her eyes half-closed as she moves her hips up and down on my cock. "I love you," she says right before her tongue slips into my mouth.

One of my hands goes to her hip while the other wraps around her back. I let her lead the pace this time, afraid that I hurt her this morning when we walked in from watching the sunrise, and she bent over in front of me. That led to her bent over the counter with one leg up as I fucked her ruthlessly. I thought she would look at me differently, afraid I hurt her, but she just looked over her shoulder after I came in her, and said, "We should do that every single morning."

She puts both hands behind her now as she picks up the pace. "So good," she says, closing her eyes, and I watch her tits rise and fall. I lick my thumb and rub it over one of her nipples, getting it hard. She moans, and her speed picks up. "Oh, god," she says. I lean forward and bite down on the nipple and then suck in, and her pussy spasms on my cock. "Yes."

"Tell me what you want?" I ask, and she just opens her eyes and looks at me and then closes them again when she sinks back down on my cock. I hold her hips down. "You won't be able to move until you tell me what you want."

She groans in frustration and then moves her hips side to side. "I have to move."

"Tell me what you want," I ask her again, my hips thrusting up to get deeper in her.

"I want to," she says as she rolls her head from one side to the other. "To make me come."

I smile now. "I can do that," I say. Releasing her hips, I lean forward, put her hand on my neck, and move up and down now faster than she did before. I lick my thumb again, but this time, I find her clit. "So close." I feel her, moving my thumb in little circles. "So close."

"Yes," she pants out, arching her back, and my mouth

catches one of her nipples and bites down. It's the last straw, and she coats my cock, calling out my name over and over again. Her arm lets go of my neck as I lay her down, my cock still buried balls deep inside her.

She wraps her legs now around my waist, and she smiles at me. "Fuck, I love you," I say as I make love to her softly and slowly until I can't wait anymore, and the thrusts get harder and shorter. We come together this time, and when I roll to the side, taking her with me, I feel her kissing my shoulder.

"Is it always this good?" She looks up at me with her hand on my chest and her chin resting in the middle of it.

"No," I answer her. "But with you..."

"Yes?" She smiles at me.

"It just gets better." I curl up and kiss her lips.

"Are we going to shower together?" I ask, slipping out of her and rolling off the bed.

"You don't have to ask me twice," she says, walking into the bathroom and starting the shower. "What time is Ethan picking you up?" she asks when I step into the shower with her.

"Soon," I say, and she turns, and I see a twinkle in her eye.

"Soon that we can't have shower sex?" She tilts her head to the side. "Or soon we can have shower sex, and I get to wash my hair."

My cock springs into action. "Soon, meaning we can have shower sex, but I can't wash your back." I lean down and take her lips.

"I can work with that," she says, and forty minutes later, I'm stepping out of the shower alone. "That was good," she says, and I laugh to myself as I grab the white towel and dry off. "Not as good as the kitchen but still okay."

I look over at her, seeing her wash her hair now. "Are you rating us?"

"Yes," she says without skipping a beat.

"What was the worst?" I ask, and I stand with my hands on my hips.

"They were never bad." She shakes her head. "There are just some times that were better than the last."

"Okay?" I lean back on the counter and fold my arms over my chest. "Which one was number one?"

"It's a tie," she answers me, rinsing her hair. "Between the first time and the kitchen table." I want to say something, but I don't because she continues talking. "Like the first time will always be special because it was the first time you touched me. But the kitchen is just..." She rubs the shower door to see me through it. "The kitchen was animalistic. It's like you couldn't stand it no more, and you just had to have me. It was hot."

"I didn't hurt you?" I ask her.

"You aren't going to break me," she says, turning off the water now. "You can't medically break my vagina. Medically, you can tear my vagina but not break it. But that only happens when someone is dry down there."

"Am I really having this conversation?" I ask, and I hear her phone ringing from somewhere in the house. "I'll be right back." She laughs.

I walk to the kitchen, but I come face-to-face with Ethan, who stands there with his phone in his hand. "I was calling."

He spots me with just a towel on. "Can you go and get dressed, please"—he shuts his eyes tight—"and I'm going to pretend that my sister isn't in the shower with you."

"I'm not in the shower." I point at myself. "I'm out of the shower." I point out to him. "Which means I'm not in the shower with your sister."

"Thank fuck," he says.

"I mean, I just left her in the shower." He groans as I walk over to my bedroom. "But I'm not in there with her now."

"Tonight, you get your own car," he says, and I walk into the room and get dressed.

When I walk back out, Ethan is sitting at the counter drinking coffee and Chelsea is dressed in shorts and a top, her hair wrapped in a towel. "I'm just starting breakfast."

"I told her we would get something on the way, but she's sturbborn," Ethan says.

"My man needs his energy," she says, winking at Ethan, and then he pushes away from the counter, making her laugh.

"And we are out," he says, and she laughs even harder. "I'm waiting in the car."

"I have to go and buy some new clothes," I say. "I have a couple of things left from what Ethan brought over."

"I can go and grab you a couple of things if you want," she says. "With Amelia." The uneasiness is hitting me in the stomach.

"I'll see if Quinn can come with you," I say, and she rolls her eyes at me. "I'll see you later."

"You bet your ass you will," she says and leans her head back for a kiss. "I'll call Quinn. He likes me better than you."

"Good call," I say, walking out of the house and going over to the truck. "She's going shopping."

"I'll get someone to trail her," Ethan says, typing something in the phone.

"She is going to call Quinn." He nods at me as we make our way to the barn.

We walk in, and Casey is there waiting for us. "Morning," I say, and he just smiles at me.

"Morning," he says. "Do you have a couple of minutes?"

Ethan slaps me on the shoulder. "I'll get that thing going."

Casey waits for Ethan to walk away from us before he talks. "How are you doing?"

"Good," I say, and he just looks at me. "I'm anxious but okay. I just want to find him and get this over with."

"Especially now that you are dating my niece." He cuts right to the chase.

"Is that going to be a problem for you?" I ask, but I don't wait for him to say anything. "Because if it is, I can continue this on my own."

"I want you to work for me," he says, and I shake my head.

"I can get my own job," I say.

"I know you can," he says, "but I need someone like you on my team." He pushes off now from the desk he was leaning on. "Come with me," he says, walking over to the room I spent all of yesterday in. He turns on the light in the room, and I see the whiteboard I was working on. "This," he says, pointing at the board where I started doing a timeline for my father. "This is what you're good at."

"There is a gap," I say, looking at the board. "For three years, he was quiet." I look at the board. "The answers are there."

"Well, if anyone can find it, you can," he says. "This is what I need." He points at the board. "Think about it," he says. "Something tells me you aren't leaving when all this is done."

He stops right before he walks out. "I'm happy for you," he says, and I look over at him. "But if I'm honest, I'm happier for Chelsea. She's loved you for a long time."

"Did everyone know but me?" I ask, and he laughs.

"No, I think you and Beau were the only ones who didn't know," he says, laughing now. "Thank you for that. I will never let him live it down." He walks out at the same time Ethan walks in.

"Quinn is with the girls," he says, handing me a cup of coffee. "He wants it on record that he took one for the team." I laugh. "He was not kidding."

"I'll put a sticker next to his name," I say, looking back at the timeline. "I want to make a couple of phone calls," I say.

"Who are you going to call?" he asks as I sit down at the big desk in the middle of the room.

"Every single neighbor he ever had during that time." I pick up a pen and start to make a list. "Someone had to have had a run-in with him. There has to be someone somewhere." I look down at the blank paper now. "If my father was there, trust me, he made enemies."

Twenty-Eight

CHELSEA

"We have to leave in twenty minutes," I say as I walk into the closet and look for something to wear. It's been three weeks since he made me his. Every single day for the past three weeks, he gets more and more on edge, and I have no idea how to make it okay for him. Three weeks without one sighting of his father. No sign of him, and I secretly wish he was dead somewhere in a ditch.

"Then stop walking around naked," he says from behind me, wrapping his arms around my waist. The only time he lets go just a bit is when we are home and locked in.

"I'm not naked," I say. "I'm wearing a thong and a bra." I turn to the side, and he kisses my lips, his tongue slipping in with mine.

"Same as being naked," he says, and I turn in his arms now. "I can't get enough of you," he says between kisses. Both of us forget we only have twenty minutes as he carries me back to bed and makes love to me.

"I can nap right now." I look over at him as he gets out of bed.

"There is no time to nap. We're already going to be late," he says. "We were late last week, too."

"Two weeks ago, we showed up at the barbecue when they were eating dessert," I remind him.

"That was your fault." He points at me. "You wanted to ride." I laugh, shaking my head.

"I did," I say, getting out of bed now and walking to the bathroom. "I'm going to take a quick shower."

"I'll text your mother this time," he says. "She is the only civil one."

I laugh at him. "They are all civil. They just like to tease you."

My family has always accepted him, even from before, but when we walked into the barbecue on Sunday at my grandparents' holding hands, there were whispers and then a couple of fingers pointing. I was nervous as hell, and I almost threw up in the car on the way there, but they treated him just like they did the last time. No one treated him any different, and I think it was a relief even to Mayson, even if he pretends it wasn't.

When I get out of the shower, he is dressed in jeans and a black shirt, his hands going nuts on his phone. "Everything okay?"

"Yeah, we are just chasing a lead," he says as I walk into the closet to put back on the thong he just took off me and the same strapless bra.

I slip on my blue jeans with holes in the middle of my thighs and one in the knee. I grab my yellow off-the-shoulder loose shirt. I slip my arms in the sleeves and tie the little bows at the bottom. I walk out, and he looks up and smiles. "You look beautiful," he says, getting up and kissing my bare shoulder. "Ready to go?"

"Almost," I say, walking into the bathroom and grabbing the necklace he gave me two weeks ago.

"Let me," he says, coming in, and I hold up my hair so he

can clasp the necklace. The heart pendant falls in the middle of my chest. I hold the heart in my hand and smile at him through the mirror. "Ready?"

"Yes," I say, walking out and slipping my cowboy boots on. I grab my purse and walk out of the house, holding his hand in mine, and we walk over to the truck he also bought two weeks ago.

I look out the window as we make our way over to my grandparents' house.

We get there thirty minutes late, and I look over at him. "We aren't that late," I say and laugh when he closes his eyes and gets out of the truck. He comes over and grabs my hand, kissing my fingers as we walk around the house to the backyard.

I smile when I see all the people here. Sunday dinners were something I always looked forward to. It was a chance for my cousins and me to get together. Quinn is talking to his brother Reed and Asher about something.

Amelia spots me and waves from across the yard as she plays with Aubrey. Her brother, Graham, along with my brothers Toby and Keith, are in the middle of the yard as they look at something on someone's phone.

"There you are," my mother says, coming to me now. "Your grandmother was looking for you." She kisses my cheek and then hugs Mayson next. "It shows that you got the clearance to go back to the gym."

"Well, it wasn't from me," I say, folding my hands over my chest. "He went to see Dr. Gabe, who gave him the okay." I mention my boss, who didn't listen to anything that I said. I thought it was too soon, but what do I know, apparently.

"You're still upset." He puts his arm around my shoulder. "I just asked him if I could hit the gym."

"After I told you no," I remind him. It was the first big

fight we had. I look down now, and think about how we made up. That is now tied up there along with the first time.

"There she is," I hear and look over to see my grandparents coming over to us, their hands intertwined together. "Hello, lovebirds." My grandmother smiles at us. "To be young and in love."

We all laugh now as Ethan comes over to grab Mayson. "Guys are taking the horses out and going over to the clearing to shoot."

"Why just the guys?" I ask Ethan, who looks over at my grandfather for help.

"Um," he says. "The women are busy cooking." He winks at my grandmother, who glares at him.

"Ethan McIntyre, you did not just say that," she hisses. "Did we teach you nothing?"

"Well, you taught me that you don't want me in the kitchen with you," he says. "The only boy you allow in the kitchen is Gabriel." He turns to Mayson. "You coming?"

"Yeah," he says and kisses me softly and then walks away with Ethan.

"He's too good looking for his own good," I say to my grandmother and then look down when I feel someone pull on my shirt and see Aubrey. "Well, hello there, beautiful girl," I say, kissing her cheek. She slaps my chest and plays with the locket. My grandparents walk to greet someone who just showed up.

"We were wondering how late you would be today." My aunt Kallie comes over now with my aunt Olivia by her side. "I had you at ten minutes."

"I had you not coming at all." My aunt Olivia laughs now.

"We aren't always late," I say and try to be serious about it. "It's only been three weeks. We were on time that first week," I say, and Amelia looks over at me.

"Your shirt was buttoned wrong." She shakes her head, and I hide my laughter.

"How is work?" my aunt Olivia asks.

"It was tough at the beginning." Last week, I started my job as a nurse at the family practice a town over. If it was up to Mayson, I would stay home until his father is caught, but I was going crazy. We compromised, and by that, I mean, I said it was okay to have someone drive me to work, sit in the parking lot, and then drive me back home. It was not only for Mayson but it was for my whole family, who were against me going back.

"Starting a new job is always scary," my aunt Kallie says. "I'm sure in a couple of weeks, it'll feel like you were there the whole time."

"There she is," Emily says, coming over to us and looking at her daughter. "Were you good?

"Where are the men?" Emily looks around.

"They went to ride horses and then shoot," Amelia says with a gruff. "Like I can't shoot." She looks at my aunt Olivia. "I'm going to shoot Quinn in the foot one of these days."

We all laugh. "Was he mean to you?"

"He was being a horse's ass," she says, and I roll my lips.

"I'll talk to him," my aunt Olivia says.

"Did they take Gabriel?" Emily says, looking around, and neither of us makes eye contact with her.

"I'm going to kill your son." She looks at my mother, taking her phone out of her back pocket and calling him, walking away from us.

"Ten minutes," I give out a number. We started this betting thing as far back as I can remember. We would always bet to see how long it would take.

"Not coming," Amelia says. "He's going to call her Sunrise, and she'll be putty in his hand."

"You need to look into becoming a lawyer," my aunt Olivia says to her.

"I say five minutes," my aunt Kallie says. "I have to have faith in my boy." Amelia and I just look at her, shaking our heads.

Emily comes back, putting her phone in her back pocket. "So what did he say?" Amelia asks.

"Well..." she says.

"Called it," Amelia says, clapping her hands together now.

"Oh, shut up," Emily says. "He is sitting on the horse with Jacob, so he's fine."

"Lies," I say and then look over at my grandmother, who is walking back into the house. "I'm going to go and help." I walk away from the women and stop to say hello to a couple of people who always come over.

I open the screen door and walk in, smelling the pies right away. "What can I do to help?" I ask her, walking over to the sink and washing my hands, even before she says anything.

"You are glowing," she says, and I look over at her. "You were always beautiful." She walks over to the oven and opens it to peek in. "But these past couple of weeks, it's just..."

"I feel like I'm complete." Does that make sense? "I know I don't need a man to complete me, but going to bed in his arms every single night." I smile. "It's the best thing in the world."

She smiles at me. "To this day, I can't sleep if your grandfather isn't next to me. He could be downstairs watching television, and I won't be able to sleep without him."

"That is so sweet." I smile now at her.

"Sweet but also annoying." She grabs her rag, opening the oven again as she takes out the first pie. "Where is the plate you took last week?" My grandmother looks over at me.

"I forgot it at home," I say to my grandmother. "I'm going to go quickly," I say. "Can I take the truck?" I walk over to the table at the front door and grab the keys.

"Don't be daft," she says. "I have a million plates."

"No, it's fine," I say, opening the front door.

"Go and get Amelia to go with you," she says, and I shake my head.

"I'll be ten minutes," I say and walk out of the house, getting in the truck and making my way back to my house.

Twenty-Nine

MAYSON

Fourteen of us got on horses and followed Quinn and Casey twenty-five minutes out, behind a forest of trees, coming out to a fenced-in opening. The sun is heating us up in record time.

A red barn sits there right at the front of the fenced area. Asher gets off his horse and walks over to the barn doors. He opens one door and then goes to open the other one. One by one, we ride in.

We all get off our horses, and I don't know why I'm expecting a small barn, but nothing Casey does is small. There are twenty stalls all ready and prepared for the horses, buckets of water sitting in each stall filled with hay. "Each horse has its own stall," Asher says. "Load them up."

I hook up my horse and walk out just in time to see Quinn walking over to a solid silver door on the right-hand side. He puts his thumb on the keypad, and you hear a click, the door opening for him. "Gentlemen and little one." He winks at Gabriel. "Are you ready to have some fun?"

"Follow me." Asher walks past us to the doors in the back.

Once I make my way out, I put my hand up over my eyes

to see what I'm looking at. It looks like a shooting range, except there are targets all over the place. It looks like over a hundred people all scattered around the place. A wooden table is set up where you would stand to shoot.

"Holy shit," Toby says. "I can see myself spending lots of time here." He claps his hands together happily.

"If you bring my son here without me"—Ethan looks over at them—"Dad isn't going to be able to save you from my foot going in your ass."

"If you bring Gabriel here"—Beau looks over at us with his hands on his hips—"I'll whip your asses myself."

"I'll help your father." Jacob now pipes in, and Toby just nods his head.

Quinn and Casey now come back out with us, each of them carrying two shotguns. "Ready to play a little game?" Quinn walks over to the table, putting down both of the guns he is carrying. "You each get five shots." He smiles. "Most hit targets wins. Easy as that."

The young kids fight over who will win, and Ethan and I just share a look, smirking at each other. I walk over, grabbing one of the folding chairs, and sit down. Ethan follows my lead as we sit down side by side.

Toby and Keith both hit five targets. Reed misses one. I'm sitting back in my chair, making a plan in my head. Quinn comes over now and takes a seat next to me. I look over at him; in the past three weeks, he's been coming around more. I mean, we aren't best friends, that is for sure, but at least we aren't at each other's throat. "I'm telling Chelsea," Quinn says, looking at me. "That you are out here shooting, and you didn't bring her."

I laugh now. "Are you trying to get into my head?" I look over at him, shaking my head, then turn back to look at Ethan as he shoots.

"Is it working?" he asks me.

"You know I went to war, right?" I say, and he rolls his eyes.

I laugh at him when Ethan calls my name. "Mayson, you're up."

I get up now, smiling at Quinn. "Watch and learn, grasshopper." Walking over to the wooden table, I try out the guns to see which one I like more. I find the one I want and look over at Ethan. "What did you get?"

"I got all of them." He holds up his whole hand. "Think you still got it?"

I laugh. "Only one way to find out." I walk over to the shooting pad. I hold up the gun now, looking through the barrel. "I'm getting ready to shoot!" I shout to make sure everyone is in the back of the line.

"Just so you know," Casey says now from beside me. "I have your file in my office."

"What does that mean?" I ask, not looking over at him.

"It means I know if you are going to throw this, just to be nice to your girlfriend's family." He chuckles.

"You obviously don't have the right file," I say, firing off a shot and hitting the first target. "Because it would tell you that I don't give a shit who I'm up against." I aim again for another target and pull the trigger. "I'll win."

I wait until my last shot to make the shot I've been thinking about. If you look over to the right, there is one target at an angle, and if you hit it in the right spot, you can hit two targets at one time. I hit it at the right spot, and the bullet goes through one and then straight into the one behind it.

"Ooohhhh!" the guys behind me all yell out.

"I knew he was going to do that," Ethan says, getting up when his phone rings. "Hey, Sunrise," he says and walks away to talk to her.

"Nice shot," Jacob says, holding up his hand to give me a high five.

I walk over to Casey, who looks at me, and smirk. "If you want..." I put the gun down on the table. "You can add that to my file."

He shakes his head. "How?" Beau says, leaning back in his chair and looking over at where I took the shot. Ethan comes back over now, sitting down in one of the empty chairs.

Walking over to the chair I was just sitting in, I lean over to Beau. "There are four other targets that you can do that with."

"No, there isn't." He shakes his head, and all the other men are looking at me, even Ethan.

I point at Ethan now. "You are getting soft." I shake my head and then hold up my hand. "Right there." I point at the two on the far left. "Right down the middle. See how they are one in front of the other, but the other is far behind?"

Quinn gets up, grabbing the guns now. "He wins." Everyone gets up, getting ready to head back to the barbecue.

"What does he win?" Gabriel asks and comes over to me. "Will you share it with me?"

"I can do better than that," I say. "You can have it."

His eyes open wide. "Thank you, Uncle Mayson," he says and runs after Quinn. "What did he win?" He hops up and down beside him.

"He won a sticker," Quinn says, looking around. "A sticker that Grandma has at the house."

"A sticker," he says, defeated.

"And the biggest piece of pie." Quinn tries to think of another cool prize.

"That sucks," he says, and we all laugh.

"Let's head back before the girls freak out," Jacob says, walking back into the barn and grabbing his horse. "I'm going to head back with the kids," Jacob says, and I look up, seeing most of the kids on their horses.

"I'll help close up here," I say, looking back to see Asher cleaning up. "Tell Chelsea."

"That you love her," Toby says. "I'll tell her." He laughs and trots out with Keith next to him.

"I'll make sure she's okay," Beau says, following Jacob in the back of the group.

I help Asher close the back doors and then look in to see the room that Quinn walked in before, and I stop in my tracks. "What in the...?" The whole room has wall-to-wall cages with guns in them. "You definitely didn't show Toby this room," I say, walking in, and Quinn laughs, shaking his head.

"You and Ethan are the only ones who have really seen it," Casey says. "If you ever want to come out and shoot."

"You could bring Chelsea out, and we can see if she has a better shot." Quinn smirks at me. "My money is on Chelsea."

"Mine, too," I say, and then we walk out of the room and get on the horses. I wait outside of the barn for Casey and Quinn to come out. Asher then closes up, and the four of us ride back. A bit faster than when we got there.

Getting back to the barn, I get off the horse and walk with Quinn back into the barn. "I'll take care of them," Asher says to us. "It won't take me long."

We leave the horses there, and we walk back out. The party is now in full swing, and even more people have shown up. "How does it get bigger and bigger?" I shake my head. "Just when I think it can't be bigger."

My eyes roam the backyard, looking for Chelsea. "You know my grandparents," Quinn says. "The more, the merrier."

"Yeah," I say, not paying attention as I look to see Jacob and Kallie now together.

I walk now to them since they are the closest. "Have you seen Chelsea?" I ask, and they both shake their heads.

"She is probably inside with Gram," Jacob says, and I nod.

I'm making my way into the kitchen when I'm stopped by Reed and his best friend, Scott. "I was just telling him," he says, "about the shot you got."

I smirk at them. "All you have to do is look before you shoot." I look around again and see people coming and going. "Have you seen Chelsea?" I ask, and they both shake their head.

I nod and then make my way two steps before Ethan comes to me, holding Aubrey in his arms. "Have you seen Chelsea?" I ask, looking around, and he does the same thing.

"I saw her a little while ago," Emily says calmly. "She must be around here somewhere," she says, and I look at Ethan, who is now looking around the yard also.

"There is my mom." Ethan points out to where Savannah is with Beau.

I jog to them. "Have you seen Chelsea?" I ask, and Savannah just shakes her head.

"She is probably inside," Beau says, and I nod, turning and making my way inside.

I pull open the door, and I'm stepping inside the house, my heart is beating so fast, it feels like it is going to jump out of my chest. I turn the corner to the kitchen and see blond hair, and just for a second, I calm down until the person turns and I see that it's Amelia.

"Hey," I say, my hands shaking now. "Have you seen Chelsea?"

"No." She shakes her head, and I'm about to go back outside when her grandparents walk back into the house.

Her grandfather is laughing now, and the minute he sees me, his laughing stops. "Have you seen Chelsea?" I look at him and see her grandmother gasp.

"Is she not back yet?" she says in almost a whisper, and the back door opens now, and Ethan and Beau come in.

"She isn't anywhere out there," Ethan says.

"She left." I look over at her grandmother. My mouth is suddenly dry as the hair on the back of my neck stands up.

"Where did she go?" The panic in me makes my whole

body shake as the back door creaks open again, and we all look over to see if, by some miracle, it's her. But it's only Kallie and Jacob. Their faces are showing the worry in them. "Where did she go?" I ask her again.

The tears start to flow down her grandmother's face as she wrings her hands. "She forgot my plate. I told her that I didn't need it." I'm already one foot out the door when everyone's phone starts going off.

I stop in my tracks, knowing that dread is coming. I stop in my tracks with this fear that rolls into me. I stop in my tracks with the rage that is so big I don't know how to rein it in. Ethan is the first one to talk. His voice is low. "Alarm was triggered at Chelsea's."

Thirty

CHELSEA

I slam the door shut behind me as I make my way over to my grandmother's truck. I know I should tell someone I'm leaving, but it'll be ten minutes at max, fifteen.

I pull out of the driveway just as four other trucks start to park. I raise my hand to say hello to them as I drive by. As I make my way back over to my house, I take in the quiet of the roads. Sunday is usually quiet in general. Everyone is usually with family, or most of them are stopping by my grandparents' house.

The sound of crunching rocks fills the truck as I pull into the driveway. Turning off the truck, I open the truck door. The soft breeze blows my hair back when I step out of the truck in my driveway. The sun is shining strong now, and I take a second to look up and feel the heat on my face.

I walk toward my front door when a movement to my side makes me jump. My heart speeds up, and I put my hand to my chest. Stopping to look at the trees moving just a touch, three birds come flying out as they chase each other. I laugh, shaking my head. "Smooth," I say, walking up the four steps to the front door.

Unlocking the door with the key, I turn the handle, and the cold air gushes out right away. I close the door behind me and toss the keys on the table at the front door. I rush to the kitchen, looking on the island where I put the crystal plate. The island is empty with only a cup on it. The sound of dripping makes me look at the sink to see the faucet dripping. I walk over and turn it off. My eyes go to the picture frame of my grandmother and me. It's tilted to one side, and one of the bottom edges is off the ledge. My hand reaches out to fix it. I look down and see one of my dish towels is on the floor right next to my feet. Bending down, I grab the towel, folding it and putting it on the counter.

I look around now and spot the plate on the kitchen table. "That's strange," I say to myself and then turn to look into the living room. Shaking my head, I walk around the island, and my foot hits one of the stools sticking out. I push it back into place and walk to the bedroom.

I don't know why I'm expecting it to be trashed, and when I walk in and see everything is exactly where I left everything, I shake my head and kick myself for being so paranoid. "Idiot," I say to myself, going to grab the plate on the table. I stop when one of the shades catches my eye.

The white fabric moves from the air-conditioning vent blowing under it. That isn't what catches my eye. It's the brown spot I focus on.

Placing the plate back down on the island, I start making my way over to it. I pick up the sheer fabric in my hand and see that the brown spot looks like a dirty fingerprint. I rub it between my fingers and look out, seeing fingerprints on the white shades. I turn my head now to look out into the house as my eyes go right and left. I turn back around now, my hand coming up to trace the fingerprints I see on the shades.

I turn now, my head screaming at me to get the fuck out of here. I reach in my back pocket to get my phone out and come up empty. "Fuck," I say as I rush over to the counter and grab the plate in my hand. Turning, I rush to the front door, pulling it open and stopping in my tracks. As the blood drains from my body, I feel my head spinning as it catches up to what is happening right now.

I gasp the minute I spot him, and the plate in my hand falls at my feet, shattering all around me. "This is going to be fun." His beady blue eyes shine with happiness and evil all at the same time. His hands reach up, and I see the dirt on them, and I blink. Everything feels like it is happening in slow motion. The only thing I can hear is my inner voice screaming at me to run.

I turn to bolt away from him, but my foot slips on the broken glass, and I fall on my knees. My hands come out instinctively to break my fall. Looking down and trying to focus on my hands, I feel the burning now and turn them over to see I cut my right hand open. My heartbeat echoes in my ears as the sound of my breathing is suddenly the only thing I hear over his menacing laughter. "Where do you think you're going?" he asks as I push myself up and try to run away from him. I don't get more than one step away from him before he grabs my bicep so hard in his hand, I yell out in pain.

He pulls me back to him to get a better grip on me, bending to whisper in my ear, "Now is that any way to say hello to the father of the man you fucked this morning?" The bile now starts to rise up my throat as he yanks my arm back even more.

His front is pressed into my back as he squeezes my arm so hard, I cry out in pain. "I have to say..." His breath floats over on my cheek. "I'm going to have fun with you." I close my eyes and try to rip my arm out of his hand. I must catch him off guard because my arm falls free from his grasp. I take two steps before his arm goes around my waist, and he picks me up. My feet are no longer touching the floor as I struggle in his arm now, squirming to get away from him. My hands grasp his one arm as I try to push him off me.

My survival skills kick in when I lean my head forward just a touch and then whip it back as hard as I can. The back of my head hits his nose first and then the sound of our heads hitting together fills the room. He groans, his arm fallling from around my waist, and I stumble forward, falling again. My head spins with pain, and I blink, seeing spots in front of me, but push on through. I get up and fall again, this time falling on my wrist so hard I can feel something inside snap.

I close my eyes for one second, but it proves to be too long when I feel his hand in my hair. He grips it in his fist and pulls back so hard, the burning starts, and I yell out again.

With my hair in his fist, he turns me around. When he is in front of me, I turn my head, and I kick out with all my might, missing him. He laughs snidely, pulling me even closer to him. He looks down at me. His eyes now roam over my face. He leans in even closer, and I try to back away from him, but with his tight grip in my hair, I don't move. "I'm going to take my fuckin' time with you." His hot, sour breath hits my face, causing my stomach to turn over. "When I'm done with you..." He smiles now, almost as if he won. It fills his whole face. "They won't even be able to piece you together."

"He'll find me." I find the words in my throat. "He'll find me, and then he'll kill you."

He throws his head back and laughs, lowering his guard one more time, giving me a chance to strike him without him seeing. I move my foot back and come up, kicking him in his balls. This time, I don't miss him. His hand opens, and he bends down to put his hand over his balls. I turn to sprint to the back door. My hands fumble with the lock, slipping from the blood dripping from the middle of my hand. "Come on, come on, come on," I cry out when I finally hear the click of the lock, then I slide the door open and yell, "Mayson!" I don't know why I yell. I know he can't possibly hear me. I'm about to take one step out the door when I hear a loud pop. "What the...?" I say, looking over my shoulder and seeing him standing there with a black gun in his hand aimed right at me.

I feel the heat run through me, and then the burning sets in. My legs give out on me, and I fall on them.

My head falls forward as I look down at the same place where we sit in the morning when we watch the sunrise. For the past three weeks, he's smiled more. He's looked up and seen the beauty in it. I gave him that, I think to myself as I feel water pouring down over my hand. I look down, seeing the drops of blood now running down my arm. "Mayson," I say his name again, this time in a whisper right before the darkness comes and takes me.

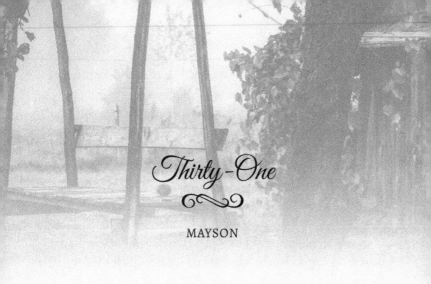

Thirty-One

MAYSON

y feet stick to the floor like glue when I hear the words over again. "Alarm was triggered." I look around the room, seeing all the men on their phone as the room starts to spin around me. I open my mouth once, but it feels so fucking heavy. I blink now once, twice, three times.

"This can't be happening," I mumble. "This isn't happening." My chest fills with a pain that I've never had before. My hand comes up to put pressure on it, hoping the pain goes away, but it doesn't. Instead, it just gets stronger and stronger.

"Mayson." I hear someone call my name, and I look over to see Ethan. "Let's go." I close my eyes and open them again. His hand goes to my shoulder. "I need you to hear my words." I look at him. "He might have Chelsea." I feel my soul detaching from my body.

"I'll kill him," I say three words. "If he touches a hair on her head, I'm going to kill him," I say, hearing commotion behind me.

"We have to get to her." I take a step, and rage fills my body as I run down the front steps and get into the truck with Ethan. I don't have a chance to close the door before he spins the truck and takes off. "Glove box," he says, and I open it to find a set of keys. "Under the seat."

I lean down and reach under the seat, grabbing the metal box. "There are two in there," he says, and my hand shakes while I slide the key into the lock and turn right. I pull open the lid and take out the two black Glocks. "They are both loaded," Ethan says as we race toward Chelsea's house.

We pull up in the driveway, and my hand is already on the handle, and I look over at him. "Take care of her," I say, knowing that only one of us will be walking out of that house, and it's going to be me, but I'll be in handcuffs for killing my father.

I get out and run toward the front door when I hear Ethan right behind me. I stop at the front door and see that it is slightly open. The door is moving with the wind now. "Ready?" He nods his head. He kicks open the door, and both of us stay back against the wall in case shots are fired at us.

Ethan holds up his hands with three fingers as he silently counts down, and when he gets to zero, I'm the first one in the house. Crunching sounds under my boots, and I look down to see shattered glass all over the place. I'm about to take one more step when my eyes fall onto the sight of smeared blood. I bend now as Ethan walks past me into the house. My hand reaches out and touches it, but the blood is already dry. "He isn't here," I hear and look up now, seeing Ethan huffing and puffing. He must have secured the house while I was on my knees. I walk into the kitchen, my eyes going all over the place.

I hear truck doors open and then close, and when I look back, all the men are here. Jacob rushes in with a gun in his hand, followed by Casey and Beau. "It's clear," Ethan says, and I look when I see movement outside, and I hold up my gun.

"It's Quinn and Asher," Casey says as I see them secure the outside.

I look to the side, and I see her shoe in the middle of the kitchen. I walk over and pick it up. "He took her."

Casey now has his phone out. "I want all the feeds from Chelsea's house on the screen in two minutes." He looks at me. "We need to go."

My heart is lodged in my throat, and an overwhelming sense of guilt rips through me as I put my head back. "Oh my god," I hear from the side and look over at Quinn, who walks into the house. "There is a pool of blood."

I'm moving even before my brain registers what he just said. He steps back out, and I look down at the spot where we sit every single day.

The pool of blood is now shining in the sun, I hear voices all around me, but I can't hear anything. The only thing I can see is the redness of her blood. "We need to go."

"I'll stay here," Asher says. "In case."

"He's not coming back here." I turn, looking at the men. Beau's face is filled with the same fear I have on mine.

Casey's phone rings in his hand, and he answers it now. "Casey," the man on the phone says.

"What do you have for me?" he says, putting his phone in the middle of the island.

"Nothing," he says. "I'm looking at the feed right now, and no one is home," he says, and I look up at his shocked face. "There has been no movement in the house since they both left three hours ago."

"I'm standing in the middle of the fucking kitchen right fucking now. Don't tell me that there is no movement in the fucking house!" he roars out.

"Casey," he says his name calmly. "I'm telling you that there is nothing on my screens."

"Then I'm telling you to fucking find out where the stream went," he says between his clenched teeth. "I got an alarm notice on my phone."

I hear the clicking of the keys in the background and wait. "Casey, there is nothing at my end. The last movement I have was at eleven fifty-six, and that is them shutting the front door."

Casey grabs his phone and opens up the alerts. "I'm sending you what I got exactly five minutes ago." My hands open and close. Has it been only five minutes?

"Someone fucked with the feed," I say, looking at him. "He had someone help him from inside."

"I would watch what you say right about now," Jacob warns me, and I shake my head.

"Watch what I say?" I roar out. "She was supposed to be protected."

"Mayson," Ethan says my name low. "We are all on the same side."

"What time did you get the notice?" I look over at Casey.

"Seven minutes ago," he says to me, and I walk to the front of the hall and lean down to touch the blood.

"Things don't make sense," I say. "The blood on the floor is dry. It takes longer than seven minutes for this to dry." I walk back to the outside and look down at the blood. "In seven minutes, it would be dry but not seeped in this much." I look over at Jacob, who comes over and checks it out.

"He's right," Jacob says. "There is no way this would be this dry in seven minutes."

"So what the fuck are you saying right now?" Beau says, his voice rising. "All I know is that my daughter is somewhere, and we don't fucking know where."

"He must have triggered the alarm," Ethan says, shaking his head, and I walk back into the house, going to the front door, and I see it now.

"He cut the wires," I say, holding it up in my hand.

"Where the fuck is the truck?" Quinn now says. "She came here in Grandma's truck."

198

"He probably took it," I say, and now Jacob gets his phone out.

"I put a GPS tracking system in it last year," he says and then talks into the phone. "I need a location for my mother-in-law's truck."

I close my eyes and then look back down at my hand that is shaking uncontrollably. "Are you going to be okay?" Quinn looks over at me, and then he asks Ethan.

"It's the adrenaline in his body," he says. "He'll be fine."

Even though he says it, I know that this isn't true. I won't be fine. I will never ever be the same. I brought this here to her. I made this happen. I put her in all of this danger. I knew I should have walked away. Knew I should have fought her every step of the way, but for once, I felt this happiness I had never known. For once, I felt like a normal person, but I should have known that this shit doesn't happen to me. It's not written in the sky for me. No matter how many fucking sunrises I look at, they will all be the same.

"Something isn't right," I say, looking around. The white curtain moves, and I walk over to it. I spot the fingerprint right away. "He was here." I shake my head. "How long was he here for before we even knew?"

"It's like he was waiting for her," Ethan says, and I turn to look at them.

"He was waiting for me," I say, looking at the men, "and instead, he got her."

"We are going to find her," Beau says, and I have to wonder if he is convincing me of this or himself.

I look over at Ethan, who is thinking the same thing I'm thinking. Both of us are wondering how much torture he is going to inflict on her. I can't close my eyes without seeing her blood. "Don't do it." Ethan comes now to stand beside me. "Don't let your mind go there."

"If I wasn't here, he wouldn't have her," I say what all of

the men are thinking. Jacob's phone rings, and I look over at him.

"They found the truck," he says. "It's about a mile from here."

We rush out of the house, everyone getting into the cars that they drove here in. My stomach flips and flops as my heart speeds up so fast it sounds like horses galloping beside me. The burning creeps up in the back of my neck. "I can't live without her," I finally say, the pain in my chest now coming back again. "She is everything."

"We are going to fucking find her," Ethan says. "Or we are going to die trying."

"When we find her," I look over at him, "I want you to take her away." He looks at me. "I want you to leave me with him." I make a list in my head now about all the things I'm going to do to him. The torture I am going to inflict on him fills my body. Shooting him will be too easy. No, not for my father. He deserves to be in hell before I finally put him there.

"She won't leave you," Ethan reminds me. "Not after all this."

I see the truck in front of us pull into a deserted road. The sound of the rocks are hitting the truck as we speed there. Tree branches slap at the windows, and we finally come to a clearing, and I see the truck there in the middle of nowhere.

I don't wait for the truck to stop before I'm jumping out of the truck and running to the truck that sits idle in the middle of the woods. "Chelsea!" I scream her name, opening the door and seeing that it's empty.

Jacob and Casey now come over with flashlights, and all we see is blood in the back seat. "Fuck!" I roar out.

I look up at the sky while the phone rings from the truck. I jump forward as I find Chelsea's phone. An unknown number flashes on the screen. I press the green button and bring the phone to my ear. "Do I have your attention yet?"

Thirty-Two

CHELSEA

The sound of the truck door opens, and I'm pulled out now. My eyes open halfway as he carries me from my grandmother's truck to a beat-up blue truck parked in a wooded area. "Let's see how long it takes for them to find the truck," he says as he opens the door to the beat-up truck. The hinges creak loudly in the silent dark forest. He tosses me on the long bench, my shoulder crying out in pain.

The driver's door opens now, making the same creaking noise as the other door did. "Let's get the fuck out of here." He starts the truck, and it rolls over. I close my eyes and pray that it doesn't start. But after three times, it finally starts up, and I close my eyes as he drives away from the truck. Every single minute, I'm getting farther and farther away from Mayson.

My body jumps every time he goes over a bump, and I float away at some point that I don't even notice when the truck stops. The creaking of the doors as they open wakes me, but no matter what I do, I can't open my eyes. I feel my legs being pulled, and then I feel like I'm floating on air. "Mayson!" I scream out in my head, but there are no words that come out. "Mayson," I say again, but this time, the only thing that comes out is a grumble.

I feel myself hanging, and when I slowly open my eyes, I'm hanging off his shoulder. The pain in my shoulder hits me right away, and I groan again. My eyes close now again, and I fight to keep them open. The sound of twigs snapping under his feet as he walks. My vision is blurry when I open my eyes again, and all I can see is the darkness of the forest. I try to spot anything that would tell me where I am.

The sound of creaking makes me open my eyes again as we walk into a wooden cabin. I look around, spotting a lone cast-iron bed in the corner. The mattress is full of stains and has no covers. He tosses me on the floor like I am a rag doll, and even though I don't want him to know I'm in pain, I can't stop the groan that escapes me. "Shut up," he hisses at me as I lie on my side, looking at him. My entire body is crying out in pain. I close my eyes, trying not to focus on the pain. Fight it back, I tell myself as I lie still, not moving.

He walks over to the table and comes back with something black in his hand. He grabs my hands together, and I cry out now in pain from my broken wrist. "Shut the fuck up," he says roughly as he zip-ties my hands together. The pain just soars through me. "Why couldn't you just shut the fuck up?" he asks, and I just look at him as he squats down in front of me. "Get up," he says, grabbing me by my hair and making me sit up, hitting my head on the wood. I don't know anything else after that because the darkness takes over. I'm standing in the middle of a forest now, and I'm running one way, and just like that, I'm taken back to where I started. I hear Mayson yelling for me and turn to go toward the sound of his voice, but I can't find him.

"Do I have your attention now?" I hear the voice in my head, and my eyes slowly open. Everything is coming back to me now. The drive to my house, the plate breaking, Mayson's father getting me. Being shot in my shoulder. I'm sitting in the dark, and the pain is kicking in. I open my eyes, but my head feels like it weighs a hundred pounds as I fall to the right and to the left. It takes everything in me to get my eyes to stay open. I fight away the darkness, knowing I have to survive this. "Now is that any way to talk to your father?"

I want to yell out and tell him not to give him anything. I want to tell him that I love him. I want to tell him not to blame himself. I want to tell him all of these things, but nothing comes out. "You want her?" he sneers at him. "Then you better fucking find her before it's too late, you son of a bitch."

He throws the phone on the counter and then looks over at me. "My boy likes you." He goes to sit in the only chair in the room. The cabin is as big as my bedroom. A counter against one wall with a sink that looks like it hasn't been used in years. A stove and fridge next to each other that looks like it's from the seventies. "He has gotten his panties all in a twist about you."

He runs his hands through his hair. "You would think he learned something from me. A woman is nothing but a warm body and a punching bag." He laughs.

I lick my lips, now tasting the metallic taste, knowing it's blood. "He's a better man than you will ever be," I croak out.

He laughs even harder now. "He's got his head up his ass if he thinks that there is something better in the world. There are no fucking rainbows. There is nothing for him, you want to know why?" I lean my head back on the wooden wall. "Because he is nothing."

I snicker now. "He is everything," I say. "He's going to find me," I say the words, and I pray it's the truth.

"I really fucking hope he does," he says. "In fact, I'm betting on it." I close my eyes, trying to talk myself out of the pain. "Thought he could hide from me for all these years." I don't say anything to him. "Ran away to the Army." He shakes his head. "Like a bitch hiding." I close my eyes now, trying to gather my strength. "Found him hiding in the woods." He laughs, getting up and walking over to a bottle on the counter. "Hiding with his tail between his legs." He swigs from the bottle and then hisses. "Boy did he squeal like a little fucking pig instead of taking it like a man."

I laugh now and open my eyes, shocking him. "How would you know what a man does?" I know that I shouldn't provoke him. "He is more of a man than you are." He gets up and comes over and backhands me before I even know what is going on. The blood now pours out from my lip, and I hear Mayson's voice in my head telling me to shut up.

"If he was a man, you would know your place," he says, trailing his finger from my cheek right down my neck and then over my breast. I close my eyes now, hoping he stops. "Make you stay in line."

He gets up now, going back over to the bottle and then sitting down. "I thought he was going to follow in my steps." My stomach goes up and down as if it's a wave in the ocean. "Made sure he watched as I took care of his mother. Kept her in her place. I kept a roof over his fucking head, and what did he do?" he hisses out. "Leaves me for dead." Takes another drink. "Took me three days to get up," he says. "Broke my fucking leg." He shakes his head now. "Left me for fucking dead," he repeats. "His own father. The one who gave him everything he has. Took in his mother when she showed up pregnant and all. Blaming me like it was my fault. Made sure the doctor took care of her for the next time. There was no way I was going to be stuck with another kid. Not me," he says, my heart breaking for the woman who suffered under his hand. "One bastard was enough."

He comes over to me now. "I'm ready," he says as his hand comes out and pushes my hair to the side. "I don't know how long I have with you." His fingers trail from my cheek to my neck, and his hand goes to the heart pendant that Mayson gave me. "Should I fuck you with the heart on?" He laughs and picks it up in his hand. "What the fuck is this?" he says and rips the chain off my neck. I watch him as he gets up and plays with the heart in his hand. "What the fuck?" he hisses, looking at me. "You fucking bitch." He snarls at me and comes over, and his hand comes out to strike me. It hits so hard that my head smashes back, and I slowly fade away, the darkness coming to get me.

The sound of crashing is all over me, and I want to scream, but the only thing I can do is let the darkness take me away.

Thirty-Three

MAYSON

E than and I move through the dark forest, side by side. Both of us geared up and ready for whatever is going to happen. The helmet on my head has the night vision goggles as we spot the deserted wooden cabin.

We sit with our backs to the tree right next to the cabin, waiting for the word to go in.

It's been the longest forty minutes of my life, standing in the middle of the forest with the abandoned truck and the phone ringing in my hand.

"Do I have your attention now?" I heard the voice, and everything in my body turned cold. I look over at Casey, who typed something on his phone.

"If you touch one hair on her head," I said with my teeth clenched so tight together I thought my jaw would break. "I am going to skin you alive."

He laughed in my ear, and all I did was clutch the phone in my hand harder. "Now is that any way to talk to your father?"

"Fuck you." The two words were the only words I could say. "You don't want her. You want me. So let her go."

"You want her." He baited me. "Then you better fucking find her before it's too late, you son of a bitch."

I took my phone and threw it against the tree. "We couldn't get a trace," Casey said, and I looked at him.

"The locket," I said the two words. "She's wearing the locket."

"Let's go." Casey turned and ran to his truck. Jacob drove as Casey got on his phone and made things happen. We were back at the shooting barn in a matter of minutes, and Quinn was the first one out of the truck as he ran toward the room.

We walked in, and he was already taking out everything we needed. "Mayson and I will go in," Ethan said, and to be honest, I zoned everything out as I got ready for the war that was going to happen.

"Okay, we got eyes on you two," Casey says into our ear. "Quinn and Jacob are right behind you."

"We are moving in," I say in the mouthpiece and then look over at Ethan. He motions to me, and we move toward the cabin. Our guns are both drawn and ready to shoot, I hear my father's voice now. "What the fuck is this?" we hear him shout. "What the fuck?" he hisses, and I look at Ethan. "You fucking bitch," he says, and when I hear him hit her, all bets are off.

"He found the tracker," I hear screamed in my earpiece. "Tracker has been found."

I get up now and kick in the door, wood flying everywhere. I make a quick sweep of the room, and my eyes fall to her as she slumps down to the floor. I feel something come over me as I charge him.

I run at him and knock him on his ass, my shoulder hitting his stomach. "You fucking bastard," I say between clenched teeth, and I sit on top of him now, my fist hitting him over and over again. "You will never," I say when my fist connects with his jaw, and I feel bones cracking, "touch her again."

I hear someone yelling my name and then feel someone grab one wrist and someone else grab the other and look over to see Ethan and Quinn. "He isn't worth it. You need to go to Chelsea."

I look over and see Chelsea slumped on the floor. I get up now and walk over to her, and my heart is in my throat as I get close to her and reach out to touch her. I move her hair away from her face and see the blood now around her mouth. A sob rips through me as I lean down and pick her up. "Baby," I say to her as she groans in my arms. "I got you."

I turn now and walk right past my father, Ethan and Quinn now standing up watching me. "Gun!" I hear someone yell, and I turn my head to the side and see that my father is holding up his hand with a gun in it.

A shot is fired, and I cover Chelsea with my body, rushing out of the house. "Shots fired." I hear Quinn in my ear as blue and red lights shine in the darkness, coming closer and closer. The lights are now filling the dark forest.

Casey and Beau both run over to us as the siren of an ambulance is right behind them. "Is she...?" Beau asks, and I nod my head.

"We have a casualty," Ethan says now in the earpiece. "Jacob took out Mayson's father."

I don't have time to think about it when the ambulance comes to a stop, and the back door opens. One of the EMTs jumps out and then pulls out the stretcher. "What do we have?" He looks at me, and I just hold her in my arms. "You have to let me at her if I am going to see what is wrong with her."

"Mayson," Beau says my name, and another ambulance gets here. Five other police cars also get here, and the lights just get brighter. People start running toward the house. Casey is on the side with a couple of people as he fills them in and starts pointing.

"I'm not leaving her." I look at the EMT, who just nods at me as I gently put her down on the stretcher. I see that her face is swollen on one side and that the yellow shirt she was wearing today is now orange. "She's been shot," I say, looking at the wound in her shoulder. My heart breaks as I look down now and see her hands tied together. "Get that off her wrists!" I shout. Beau just stands next to me, and I have to wonder if it's to keep me calm. To make sure that I don't stop them from touching her.

They cut the black zip tie off her hands, and she groans. I bend beside her. "I'm here," I say, the tears pouring out of me. "I'm right here, and I'm not leaving, do you hear me?" I kiss her lips now. "Open your eyes, Chelsea," I beg. "Please open your eyes." I put my forehead on hers, my eyes making sure her chest goes up and down. "I need to see your eyes." I see her finger move just a twitch. "I'm here, you're safe."

She groans out again, and I step back to see she is trying to open her eyes. "Mayson," she groggily says my name as she tries to move her head from right to left. The right side of her face is red from when he hit her. I look over at the cabin and think I would have gone back in and finished him.

"I'm here," I say, trying not to touch her. Her eyes now slip open but then close again when it gets too bright for her.

"We have to move," the EMT says, and I move aside as they load her up in the ambulance.

I'm about to step inside the ambulance with her when Quinn's voice comes out over the radio.

"There is another body in here. She's barely alive."

Epilogue One

CHELSEA

Six Months Later

"Where have you been?" Mayson says as I walk into the house. I look over at him and smile.

"I was at work," I say. "Where I was supposed to be."

"But," he says, looking at his watch, "you finished an hour ago."

I look at him as he stands there with his hands on his hips. My beautiful man has not left my side for more than three hours in six months. I walk to him and wrap my arms around his neck. "I said I had errands."

"No, you didn't," he says, pulling me to him. "I was worried."

"You have a tracker on my phone," I say. "You have a tracker on my truck. You have a tracker in my purse. You put a tracker in my engagement ring." I hold up the hand that has my engagement ring. I wish I could say he got down on one knee, but he didn't. After I got to the hospital, I was rushed to surgery for the gunshot wound and for them to fix my wrist.

When I finally came to, there was a ring on my finger. "Plus, don't think I don't see the car following me."

"I'm not going to apologize for keeping you safe," he says, kissing my lips and looking down.

"I'm fine," I say. I'll sometimes wake during the night and find him watching me. Even though the bruises have faded and everyone is healthy, he lives with the nightmare.

"I'm going to need visual proof." He smirks, and I shake my head and laugh at him.

"Can I get some water before?" I say, and he looks at me weird. "What?"

"What are you hiding?" he says, and I just shake my head and avoid his eyes. I open the fridge, hoping he lets it go.

"Do you want to have spaghetti for dinner?" I ask, grabbing the sweet tea and pouring myself a glass.

"Chelsea," he says, and I look at him, putting the glass down. My hand shakes, and he sees it. "Where did you go?"

"I was at work," I say, not lying. "I went for some blood work," I finally admit, pulling up my sleeve and seeing the purple mark now. If I knew there wouldn't be a mark, I wouldn't have told him.

"Why?" His voice sounds worried.

"It's nothing," I say as my palms get sweaty now and my bottom lip starts to tremble. "It's just..." I look at him, hoping this doesn't push him over the edge. "I'm late." He just looks at me, confused. "Like, my period is late."

"How long have you known?" he asks, not moving from his side of the island.

I look down, trying to calm myself. "Two weeks," I say the truth.

His eyes go big as his mouth opens and closes. "Why didn't you tell me?"

I take a deep breath and walk around the island and stand in front of him. "I was afraid."

"What?" he cuts me off with a whisper. "You were afraid of me?" The horror is in his voice as he looks at me with tears in his eyes.

"Never." I shake my head. "I was..." I wring my hands. "I didn't know how. We never spoke about kids."

"Are you?" he asks, and I smile as big as I did when they told me the news, putting my hands to my stomach. He comes to me now as the tears I tried to keep inside roll down my cheeks. He puts his hand on my stomach. "A piece of you," he says now in almost a whisper, "and a piece of me."

"I know that it's sudden," I say, "and nothing like we were expecting."

"I love you," he says, his eyes still on my stomach as his hand rubs side to side. "I promise our child will never doubt the love I feel for them and for you. Our child will know what kindness and respect is. Our child is never going to see the things I saw growing up. I promise you that."

I put my hand to his cheek. "Our child is the luckiest child in the world." He looks up at me now. "Because he is going to have you as a father."

"My heart," he says, getting on his knees now in front of me. "You have my heart." He looks up at me. "For the rest of my life until my last dying breath, you have my heart."

Epilogue Two

MAYSON

Five Years Later

"Why are you bringing her flowers again?" my four-year-old son, Tucker, asks me as we walk back to the house from the barn. It was flowers I picked along the way today as we rode our horses.

"Because I love her," I say, and he slips his hand in mine. I didn't know what love was when I met Chelsea, and then when I held my child in my arms, there was an unconditional love I felt for both of them that I couldn't even put into words. He was swaddled in a blue blanket with his eyes looking into my soul. His life was a blank canvas, and I promised to make sure it was filled with all the colors in the rainbow.

"Is that why you are always kissing her?" he asks, and I look down, seeing the little cowboy hat on him.

"Yes," I answer him, "and I like to see her smile." He nods at me as if he is actually getting all of this. But I know better than that because he asks me this question every time I pick her flowers.

"There's Mom," I say, pointing at our back door. She pushes open the door and steps out, the wind blowing in her hair. Her face lights up with a smile as Tucker lets go of my hand and runs to her. "Mommmm!"

She walks down the steps now and squats down to grab him in her arms. She hugs him close and kisses his neck as his laughter fills the yard. Another thing my son has that I never did—he smiles all the time. She puts him down now and puts her hand on her pregnant stomach.

My wife is the most beautiful woman in the world, but when she is pregnant, she is radiant. "Hi," she says when I get close enough. I kiss her lips now and hold up the bouquet. "These are so pretty." She brings them to her nose. "Shall we go and put these in water?" She looks at Tucker, who is already walking up the stairs. She turns and starts to walk up the steps with Tucker. "You coming with us?"

"In a minute," I say, and she smiles and walks inside. I walk up the steps and look at the sun that is slowly setting. It's something that I do all the time. The back door opens again, and I feel Chelsea put her hand on my shoulder. She sits next to me, and I wrap my arm around her. "Isn't it beautiful?" I ask her.

"It really is." She leans in and kisses my lips. And there on the steps where I found what happiness was, my heart beats in a whole different way.

Also by Natasha Madison

Southern Wedding Series

Mine To Have

Mine To Hold

Mine To Cherish

Mine To Love

The Only One Series

Only One Kiss

Only One Chance

Only One Night

Only One Touch

Only One Regret

Only One Moment

Only One Love

Only One Forever

Southern Series

Southern Chance

Southern Comfort

Southern Storm

Southern Sunrise

Southern Heart

Southern Heat

Southern Secrets

Southern Sunshine

This Is

This Is Crazy

This Is Wild

This Is Love

This Is Forever

Hollywood Royalty

Hollywood Playboy

Hollywood Princess

Hollywood Prince

Something Series

Something So Right

Something So Perfect

Something So Irresistible

Something So Unscripted

Something So BOX SET

Tempt Series

Tempt The Boss

Tempt The Playboy

Tempt The Hookup

Heaven & Hell Series

Hell and Back

Pieces of Heaven

Heaven & Hell Box Set